LUNATICS
AND LUCK
The Raven Mysteries

Also by Marcus Sedgwick for older readers

Blood Red, Snow White
The Book of Dead Days
The Dark Flight Down
The Dark Horse
Floodland
The Foreshadowing
The Kiss of Death
My Swordhand is Singing
Revolver
White Crow
Witch Hill

The Raven Mysteries

Flood and Fang
Ghosts and Gadgets
Lunatics and Luck
Vampires and Volts
Magic and Mayhem

For more information visit –

www.marcussedgwick.com

www.ravenmysteries.co.uk

Book 3

MARCUS SEDGWICK

Illustrated by Pete Williamson

Orion
Children's Books

First published in Great Britain in 2010
by Orion Children's Books
Paperback edition first published in Great Britain in 2011
by Orion Children's Books
a division of the Orion Publishing Group Ltd
Orion House
5 Upper St Martin's Lane
London WC2H 9EA
An Hachette UK Company

5 7 9 10 8 6 4

The Orion Publishing Group's policy is to use papers that are natural, renewable and recyclable products and made from wood grown in sustainable forests. The logging and manufacturing processes are expected to conform to the environmental regulations of the country of origin.

A catalogue record for this book is available from the British Library.

ISBN 978 1 4440 0188 4

Printed in Great Britain by
CPI Group (UK) Ltd, Croydon, CR0 4YY

www.orionbooks.co.uk

For Ann

One

Castle Otherhand
is home to
all sorts of
oddballs, lunatics
and fruitcakes.
It's just as well
for all of them
that they have
a secret weapon:
he's called Edgar.

Aaaaark!

I think I'm going grey. Yesterday I found two grey feathers in my tail, and today three more on my little black belly. I say 'little' but I am wondering if it's not as little as it used to be. I've been doing a lot of standing sideways and gazing into the mirror, and if I breathe in it doesn't look too bad, but a bird can only hold his breath for so long before he goes lightheaded, sees stars, and falls off the mantelpiece, and that sort of thing can lead to trouble. Trouble with monkeys, for a start.

I suppose I might be getting on a bit, but you know, it's not the years, it's the *damage* this place does to me.

For example, I doubt I would have any

grey feathers at all were it not for the frequent trauma and horrors I am subjected to living at Castle Otherhand, not to mention the general oddness that infects the old stones from time to time.

I'm speaking of weirdness here; peculiarities, kookiness and outright lunacy, and I can think of no greater example of this than the most dubious and downright barking series of events that recently occurred.

It all began on the day of the earthquake.

I call it a quake, out of politeness, but if its back were turned I would whisper that it was really only a tremor. Nevertheless, it was terrifying.

There was no warning.

It was a calm and sunny spring morning, the lambs were bouncing vertically in the pastures above the lake, fluffy bunnies were to be seen skipping through the daffodils at the edge of Otherhand Wood, and birds smaller and stupider than me were flying round in circles, showing off to the lady birds.

I was perching on the High Terrace with the children, striking noble poses and gazing out across the valley, giving the impression that I was full of thoughts about the deep and meaningful things in life to anyone who might care to notice. No one did.

Solstice was sitting in a wickerwork chair that she'd borrowed from her mother's room, feet crossed on the table, a large book with the word 'Spells' on the cover propped in her lap.

Cudweed was trying to tie bells to Fellah's tail so that the blasted monkey would not be able to sneak up on anyone any more; a nasty trick he had just learned and which was giving him much childish pleasure.

The twins were trying to use each other as mounting blocks to climb onto the terrace parapet so that they could continue to exercise the death wish they seem to have been born with.

All was lovely, and then there was a sudden but overwhelming smell of bad eggs.

'Oh, Fellah!,' Cudweed said, wrinkling his nose, and I have to say that the monkey almost had the pride to look offended.

But the stink was soon forgotten, as a great and thunderous rumble broke over the valley

from the mountain behind the castle. There was a second of quiet, and then everything began to wobble.

High Terrace, castle, chairs, table, children both small and large, monkey and raven alike, everything began wobbling like a jelly.

It lasted perhaps fifteen seconds, twenty tops, but I assure you the whole thing was at the same time both really scary and really, really odd.

'Solstice?' wailed Cudweed, throwing himself under the picnic table.

Solstice herself had a puzzled look on her face, and then slipped out of the wickerwork chair.

Fellah set off at a million miles an hour, or something close to it, off over the rooftops of the castle, never to be seen again. Or so I hoped.

The twins rolled around on their backs, giggling and waving their legs in the air, and I decided the safest place to be was in the air, which I was pleased to find, wasn't wobbling.

Then it was over.

'What . . . ?' wailed Cudweed, from under the table. 'What . . . ?'

Solstice picked herself up from the flagstones, and adjusted the hem of her black velveteen dress.

'Ooh!' she said. 'Cudweed! Oooh! I think we just had an earthquake! The earth has ruptured! Releasing stinky sulphurous gases and making everything wibble-wobble . . . Let's go to the kitchens and see how much has been broken!'

She ran off excitedly, but Cudweed only stuck his head out from under the table.

'No,' he said. He sounded very determined. 'I'm not coming out.'

The boy had a point, I thought. If I had been an earth-bound creature I might also have opted to stay underneath the nearest piece of furniture, but since I am a master of the skies, I decided to stay where nothing could fall on me.

I soared up, away from the High Terrace, keeping one eye on the twins who appeared to be waiting eagerly for the whole thing to happen again, and from on high I saw that the whole valley was quiet and still. Every creature had bolted for cover, every bouncy lamb and skippy bunny, even the smaller and stupider showy-off birds were quaking out of sight in their nests.

I alone was the Lord of All Creation.

And then I heard a tinkling sound, tiny and tinny, but nonetheless, a definite tinkling sound. It was, I realised after a moment's reflection, the sound of a bell, and once the cogs turned in my brain a bit more, I understood its source.

The monkey.

The monkey was hopping and lolloping back across the rooftops, heading for home in Cudweed's room.

I should have known there and then that something was wrong, but at the time I just thought it odd that the idiotic primate was using only three of his limbs to skip along. I think I dimly hoped he had hurt himself, but that was it.

Little did I know then that I had just witnessed the start of all the weirdness.

Two

Solstice's best-ever birthday involved a troupe of acrobats, a chocolate fountain, a dancing bear and a trampoline at midnight. Though not all at the same time. That would be silly.

'Whaaaaaaaaat?' roared Valevine.

He was in quite the worst mood I had seen him in for a very long time. This was because, of all the parts of the castle that had been damaged by the earthquake, his laboratory high in the East Tower seemed to have fared the worst.

He and Flinch had been engaged in quite the most desperate battle for knowledge ever undertaken by the human mind, or so he said. They'd been conducting experiments into why chocolate ice cream is quite so scrummy, but when the wobbling began, all nine bowls of the stuff had been sent crashing to the floor, where they were now seeping stickily down between the cracks in the flags.

'Everything is ruined!' Valevine had declared, storming down the spiral staircase. He had called an emergency assembly of the entire family in the Small Hall, and had just asked Cudweed to explain the cause of earthquakes.

The small and wretched child had mumbled something so inaudible as to be positively annoying.

'What?' repeated Valevine, again at full terrifying volume. 'What did you say, boy?'

Cudweed gulped.

'I wondered if it's to do with the moon. Most things are, aren't they? Aren't they?'

Valevine's face was terrible to see.

'The moon? Pah!'

He whirled round and, still furious about the melting ice cream, accosted Solstice.

'You, oh daughter of mine, what do you have to say for yourself? What are the causes of the phenomenon we know as the earthquake?'

Solstice fiddled with her necklace, a charming thing with death heads and whatnot.

'Erm, well,' she said, 'I think it's something to do with plate tectonics, isn't it?'

I put my head under my wing, dreading Valevine's reaction. So I didn't see his face, but I heard him explode.

'Plates! Plates? Are you trying to be funny?'

'No!' cried poor Solstice. 'I just read something about the Earth's crust rubbing against itself, and . . .'

'Enough! You're only making it worse for yourself, Daughter!' Valevine cried. He stomped

about the Small Hall for a bit, kicking a few polar bear rugs in the backside as he did, while everyone else stared at their shoes and coughed quietly.

'Right!' he cried. 'That's it! I have made a decision. No! I've made two decisions!'

Now at this point there was a bit of fuss. The coughing stopped and turned into muttering, because one thing that Valevine is infamous for is his decisions. The castle tends to run in fear of him actually deciding something, rather than just muddling along in the usual way.

For example, there was the time Valevine decided that wings were unnecessary for flight, and that determination would do. I could have told him. Fortunately he also decided to try his experiment over water, so when he'd dog-paddled back to the shore of the lake, it was only his pride that was hurt, as he seemed to have missed the mysterious creature that lurks in the lake's murky depths.

Then there was the time he decided that everyone in the castle should stay awake for as long as they could, 'to see what happens'. What happened was that everyone got very tired, then very grumpy, then started thinking they were made of cheese, or that they were the Queen of Cyprus, or an elephant in pyjamas. Then everyone fell asleep for a week and woke up chewing the carpets where they lay.

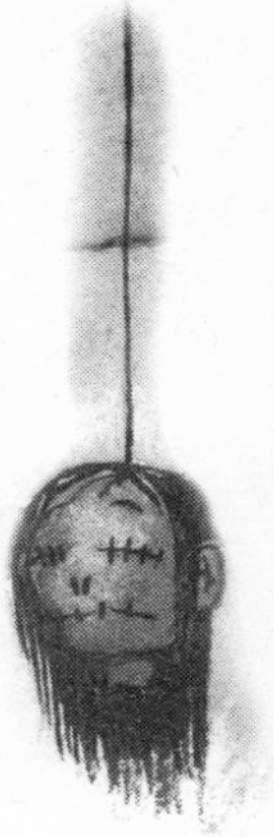

And there was the time that he decided ravens were evil birds that shouldn't live in people's homes. His worst idea ever, and one I soon set him straight on when the entire rest of the family sided with me in trying to have him thrown out of the castle instead.

So when Valevine announced he had made not one but two decisions, there was understandable commotion.

'Decision number one!' Valevine announced, his eyebrows twitching wildly.

'It is obvious to me, as never before, that we live in perilous times. At any moment, the castle could come crashing down around our ears as a result of earthquake, tidal wave, or all the rabbits in the meadow jumping at exactly the same time as all the lambs. We cannot live with this uncertainty, and therefore, as much as it pains me to do so, I am going to put aside my research into ice cream, in order to build a machine to predict the future!'

There was a moment's silence, and then, surprisingly, a huge round of applause. It took me a minute to work out why. Everyone had simultaneously realised that this decision of Lord Otherhand's would affect precisely no one but himself. And Flinch of course, who was indeed the only one in the room not cheering with relief.

But then!

Oh, then came Valevine's second decision, and it was terrible indeed, even though once again it only affected two people in the castle.

Those two people were Cudweed and Solstice.

'I have also decided,' he belted out into the air with menace and determination, 'that my children's education is shabby, appallingly sketchy, and, dash it all, non-existent. I am therefore going to place an advertisement in the paper for a private tutor in order that they may receive some decent and proper instruction.'

'No! Father, no!' wailed

Solstice and Cudweed as one.

'Yes! Children, yes! You are going to have a schoolmaster, and you will learn something, by golly, or I'll want to know why not!'

Now once again, everyone else in the room was secretly rather relieved that the pronouncement had nothing to do with them, but I must say I felt rather sorry and a touch cross for the children. Education is a simply awful business, I recall from my dim and distant youth, and as always, I felt a touch of horror at someone new entering the castle.

But while I was contemplating these matters, and Cudweed and Solstice were clinging to each other for moral support, and everyone else was slinking away hoping that Valevine wasn't about to add a third decision, something most odd occurred.

A coin, from out of nowhere it seemed, bounced down the main stairs and landed between the rugs in the Small Hall. It hit a table leg and began to spin around as coins like to do, and it was such an odd thing that everyone stopped and watched.

Then the coin did something odder, because rather than fall on one side or the other, heads or tails, if you see what I mean, it stopped spinning and remained standing on its edge.

'Coo,' said Cudweed. 'That's weird. You couldn't do that if you tried. I bet,' he went on,

getting quite excited, 'if you lived to be a thousand years old, and did that a hundred times a day till you dropped dead, you'd never manage to do that again.'

Which was an interesting thing to say, because just then another coin appeared, also as if from nowhere, and bounced down the steps, and hit a table leg, and spun around. And then stayed standing on its edge.

'Coo.'

That was Cudweed again, and his voice was no more than a whisper.

'That's . . . weird,' said Solstice.

And so it was.

But it was nothing compared to the weirdness that was to follow.

Three

Everyone knows that Minty's real name is Euphemia, but few people know that she was named after her grandmother, Euphemia Summersby Bolpox, the witchiest witch for over two centuries.

In the aftermath of the earth wobbling, the castle became mysteriously quiet. There was a lot of sweeping and picking up of things to be done, throwing out of broken china and what-have-you, and then everyone disappeared. I know this because I flew the length and the breadth of the castle and didn't see a soul.

Solstice had in fact locked me in my cage in the Red Room, but, as you may know, I never spend long in there before flicking the secret catch and letting myself out again. As I explored the apparently deserted corridors, I realised that the castle itself seemed to be holding its breath, as if another earth-wobbling might start at any moment. Not a board creaked, or door groaned, or curtain flapped.

Everything was still.

So!

I decided to find out where everyone had got to.

I started at the top of the castle and the East Tower. I settled on the windowsill outside Valevine's laboratory. There was silence.

No banging, no whizzing or fizzing, no whirling or hammering. Nothing.

Most odd. But as I looked in, I could see Valevine sitting at the lab table, among the broken bits and pieces of what he liked to call scientific equipment. His back was towards me but I could see that he was writing furiously.

I left him to it.

I found Minty sitting on her bed, reading a book about sculpture, her latest obsession.

'Ah, Edgar,' she said, when she saw me hop onto the rug. 'Still here?'

I think that was meant to be a joke of sorts, but I just hopped onto the bed and peered at the pictures in the book.

Most odd, I thought again, the things humans spend their time doing. Given the choice, I would not spend two years hitting a piece of rock with a chisel to make it look like a bad imitation of a person. I would rather eat dried mice and sleep a lot. But then maybe I'm not as ambitious as I once was.

I left her too, and went in search of the young humans. I flew down the corridor, passing the nursery with a shiver, even though I gathered that the dreaded Nanny Lumber was on her annual holiday. She'd gone to some nannying conference, a special meeting where she would learn how to be more vicious and evil, I presume. That made the nursery a safe place for once, but I knew the twins would be nowhere near it anyway.

Sure enough, I found them crawling along the banisters on the fifth floor landing, somehow only ever falling onto the carpeted side, not the side with the five-floor drop to a hard stone floor. Uncanny knack, it's true, but maybe they were just born lucky.

That thought would come back to me later.

Nevertheless, I spent half an hour doing funny little dances and wing flaps to draw them away from death-defying banister antics and lure them back down the corridor towards the safer realms of Solstice's room, where I found Cudweed and Solstice staring very gloomily into space.

The monkey was absent, but that was not the cause of Cudweed's misery, and neither was it the origin of Solstice's woes.

She looked up as I hopped through the doorway.

'Didn't I put you in your cage?' she asked.

I shrugged, which never comes out that well since I don't have much to offer in the shoulder department, but I think she got the point.

The point was, yes, you might have, but you don't actually expect me to stay there, do you?

'Oh, Edgar,' Cudweed wailed. 'What are we going to do?'

I hopped over to the poor boy, who sat with his knees pulled up to his chin, or as close as they could get to his chin given that he's a bit too fond of chocolate cake.

'**Urk?**' I asked.

'Yes, Edgar, that's right,' he moaned. 'Do you know where Father is? Right now, he's up in his room, writing. And do you know what he's writing? That's right. An advertisement! And you know what it's an advertisement for? Yes, that's also right. A teacher. A school teacher, for us.'

'And,' added Solstice, 'you know how we feel about school teachers, don't you, Edgar?'

I did.

I ran through the last three or four the children had had.

Mrs Elbow, for example, who had left after frequent assaults by a small stroppy monkey.

Or Mr Barkworthy, who had been reduced to hysterical laughter after three weeks of Solstice answering the question before the one he was actually asking.

Then there was Miss Quick, who had run screaming from the castle one day after Cudweed, who'd taken rather a shine to her, showed her his collection of dead rodents. I gather it was Cudweed's remark, 'Don't you like their little black toes?' which had finished her off.

And there was a couple, whose names I

cannot now recall, who came as man and wife to teach our little darlings, but who made a trip into the caves one day and never returned. All we found was a textbook with a tentacle wrapped around it, pulled off in some ghastly struggle with arithmetic, we assumed.

It had indeed been a fair while since the children had last had what Valevine liked to call formal education, but I must admit that I myself stepped in to lend a hand. I like to think it was I who helped develop Solstice's interest in herbal preparations. For instance, it was I who showed her the best place to find henbane in the gardens.

And likewise, it was I who encouraged

little Cudweed's fascination with rodent skeletons, and if I got a free dinner into the bargain, then so be it.

Furthermore, it had been hard to keep finding new teachers, for one thing, and for another, the family's fortunes were running dangerously low, and the few applicants had been asking for big sums, given the Otherhand reputation.

'Maybe,' Solstice said, 'we can have one last go at pleading with him before he does anything . . . foolish.'

Cudweed sighed.

'What's the point?'

'It might be worth a try,' Solstice persisted. 'I wonder . . . exactly how miserable can you look?'

'How about this?' Cudweed said, and pulled the most extraordinarily woeful face I have ever seen. For a brief moment, he looked like a depressed camel. In fact, he looked like a depressed camel who'd been given a bad haircut.

'That might just do it,' Solstice said, grinning. 'Come on!'

She jumped to her feet and we all sped from her room, and as it turned out, our timing was, as luck would have it, perfect.

There was Valevine!

He was standing waving the wording of his advert at Flinch.

'Here you go, my man,' he announced. 'This will put an end to ignorance in my offspring once and for all! Take this to that newspaper man in town and have him print it quarter of a page. No! A half page! No, wait! A whole page! I want every school teacher in the land to beat a path to our door, and beg to teach my brainless progeny!'

'A whole page will be somewhat . . . expensive, sir,' Flinch dared to suggest.

Lord Otherhand's moustache twitched slightly, but he held his nerve.

'So be it!' he snapped.

'No, Father!' cried Solstice and Cudweed together, and then Cudweed added, 'We don't mind being stupid, anyway. At least I don't, and Solstice is really clever. Really.'

But it was too late.

At a solemn command from Valevine, Flinch strode to the front door, and flung it wide.

What happened next was the damnedest thing.

As Flinch flung open the door, a man on the other side jumped high in the air in surprise. His hand, however, remained where it had been, about to knock on the door. His mouth gaped in an expression of surprise.

He was a bit too hairy in places, I thought, but I was too

polite to mention it, and he was not what you would call tall. In fact, he gazed straight into somewhere halfway up Flinch's chest. His eyes narrowed slightly following the surprise, and he even had the nerve to try some kind of smile, though it was a smile from the grins and leers end of the scale. Behind him on the driveway sat a large wooden travelling trunk.

'Who the devil are you?' Valevine said, stepping forward, his eyebrows twitching madly yet again.

The man took a step forward to greet him, and for a small man, spoke with quite a deep voice.

'Mr Melvin Brandish,' he said. 'Travelling educationalist. You're not, by any chance, in need of a schoolmaster in this household, are you?'

'Coo,' said Cudweed.

'Gasp!' said Solstice. 'That's so weird.'

'Flinch,' whispered Valevine, out of the side of his mouth. 'Scrap the ad.'

He stuck out his hand to Mr Brandish.

'Do come in . . . Flinch! Dust off the teacher's room! Children! Say hello to your new teacher.'

Four

At the age of five Solstice fell down a deep, deep and long-abandoned well in the castle grounds. While everyone else ran around panicking, and finding ropes and ladders, she wrote her first poem. It was called, *Gasp, Isn't it Dark?*

There's a thing called hindsight, which does not refer to looking at people's bottoms, as I suspect Cudweed thinks it might.

It's a thing that means that once something has happened, it's very easy to see that it has happened, and what the consequences have been. It's harder to see things as they are happening, and it's hardest of all, I think you might agree with me, to see things that haven't yet happened at all.

Still with me?

Good. Because this sort of stuff can bend your brain fairly rapidly, I have found. Especially if your brain is small and hidden in a black-feathered brain case.

Now, here's the thing about hindsight.

With hindsight, it would have been easier

to have worked out what the hooting-heck was going on during this most curious episode in Otherhand history. The fact that a schoolmaster was half a second away from knocking on our very front door just when Lord Valevine was looking for one was a very strange coincidence.

The children were thrown into greater fits of gloom, and slunk off to their rooms hoping to avoid lessons for as long as possible, wary of a sudden surprise maths test, for example.

I flapped on to the bust of Lord Deffreeque which jutted into the air of the Small Hall, and watched the arrival of the new teacher.

I didn't like him.

He strode in rather too smartly for one thing, then looked up and saw me watching him.

'You appear to have vermin in your house,' he stated to Valevine.

'Oh? Oh, that's just Edgar. Don't mind him.'

I could feel a bad mood coming on, and turned my back on the two of them. I did, however, keep one eye trained on the scene below.

'Could I have a little help with my luggage?' Brandish enquired, pointing at the large wooden trunk.

Valevine called Flinch over and had him send for a boot–boy, Will was his name.

I say was, because he was flattened irreparably when the trunk he was carrying dropped on him half way up the stairs.

Brandish went balloon-folding barmy.

'Watch what you're doing, you clot!' he cried, and ran to stroke the trunk, checking for damage. The clot, Will, was in no position to watch anything, but Brandish seemed oblivious to that fact. By a small miracle, the trunk was as unharmed as Will was squashed, and Brandish regained his somewhat cocky air again.

Another boy was sent for, this one by the name of Joe, and he completed the installation of the trunk in the room previously set aside for school masters and mistresses.

On his way back downstairs, poor

unfortunate Joe slipped on a little goo left from the previous accident and fell to a horrible death on a suit of armour on the third floor landing. Spiky. Ow.

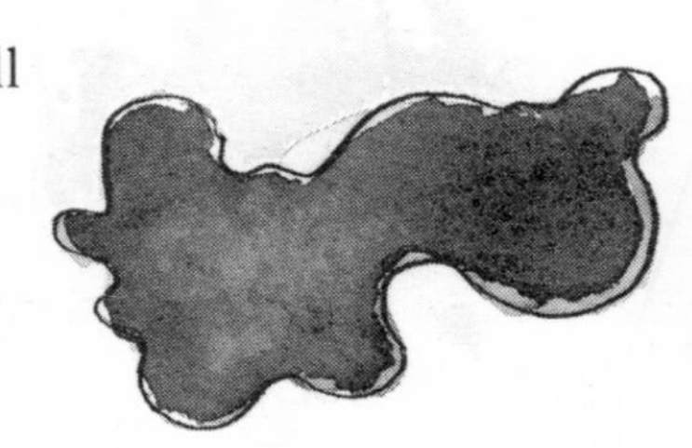

Minty arrived, and there was at once a row betwixt her and her dear husband. It was one of those furious but whispered rows that the participants believe will not be overheard by anyone else. Wrongly, of course.

'My, my!' said Minty. 'The man's only been in the place five minutes and we're two bootboys down! They're not cheap, you know!'

Valevine's moustache twitched again.

'I know that, my dear, but it was just an unfortunate accident.'

'It was two very unfortunate accidents,' Minty said.

'Just bad luck,' said Valevine.

Minty swept off upstairs to find Mr Brandish, joining him at the threshold to his room.

'What have you got in there?' she asked, tapping the lid of the trunk with her fingernails.

'Oh, clothes. You know. A toothbrush. Couple of Latin primers.'

Brandish grinned eagerly, ushered Minty out of the room, and shut the door in her face.

A second later the door popped open again.

'First lesson is Geography, nine o'clock tomorrow morning.'

The door closed, and Minty was left inspecting the woodwork.

'Do you want any supper, Mr Brandish?' she called, but there was no reply.

Having sorted the question of his children's schooling, Valevine had lost interest in the business and had disappeared back to the East Tower.

And it was there that he began to work on something that he said would put an end to the whole hindsight thing for good. Namely, his machine for predicting the future, whether that future was impending earthquakes, or teachers with lethally heavy trunks.

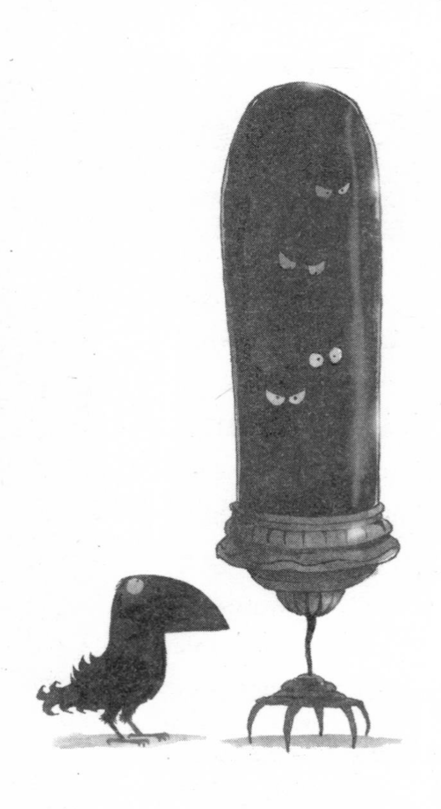

Five

It was Minty, Lady Otherhand, who chose Cudweed's name, and silly though it is, it could have been a whole lot worse. He was nearly Bramble, or Satchel, or worst of all, Squillikins.

There's a room at the top of the castle set aside for educational activity. Now it hadn't seen much activity of any sort in a fair while, as I think I mentioned. However, at nine o'clock next morning, Solstice and Cudweed traipsed into this small and rather dismal chamber like two convicted prisoners on their way to the gallows.

I flew down the corridor behind them, and my heart went out to them, especially Cudweed. Being the slower of the two, I knew this was going to be most painful for him, and secondly, I knew he'd only had time for one breakfast, rather than his usual two or three.

The room had been dusted off, as Valevine had instructed, and Brandish had clearly been there for a while preparing his instruments of torture. Pens, pencils, exercise books and other teaching materials were placed neatly on the two wooden desks at which the children would sit.

As Solstice and Cudweed dragged themselves over the threshold, Brandish looked up and with a stony face uttered a single word.

'So.'

Then, just as I was about to drift in after

them, he slammed the door in my face.

Nasty habit. I made a mental note to detest Brandish heartily until given a very good reason not to.

Not so fast, I thought, and given that there is very little I let get in my way, I set off down the corridor and with a few rather tasty beats of the old black wings I was soon speeding like a feathery cannonball. I twisted this way and that, and tilted my beak up towards a little crevice I happened to know about.

It is, after all, my business to know all the crevices in the castle, and the nooks. And the crannies. Anyway, I found myself in a rather dark and crawly space, but I saw light ahead, and a few careful clawsteps later I was peering down on the classroom from a beam way above the head of the new teacher.

Unseen, I witnessed the beginning of the abuse.

'You, boy,' Brandish was saying. 'You look rather slow and dim. What's your name?'

'Cudweed,' said Cudweed.

'You'll mind your language in my classroom, boy!' Brandish roared with sudden anger.

'But that's his name,' Solstice said, leaping to her brother's defence.

'What is?' asked Brandish.

'Cudweed,' said Solstice.

'The same goes for you!' the short and hairy teacher declared. 'I won't have profanity in my classroom! Both behave yourselves, or there'll be extra Greek homework.'

'But that's my name!' Cudweed said.

'What is?'

Cudweed opened his mouth, then shut it again. He hardly dared risk another tirade.

'My name,' he said, very quietly and quickly, 'is Cudweed and if you don't like it then you can ask my parents why they called me it.'

Brandish stared at him, then turned to Solstice.

'Is this true, girl?'

Solstice nodded.

'And what, dare I ask, is your name?'

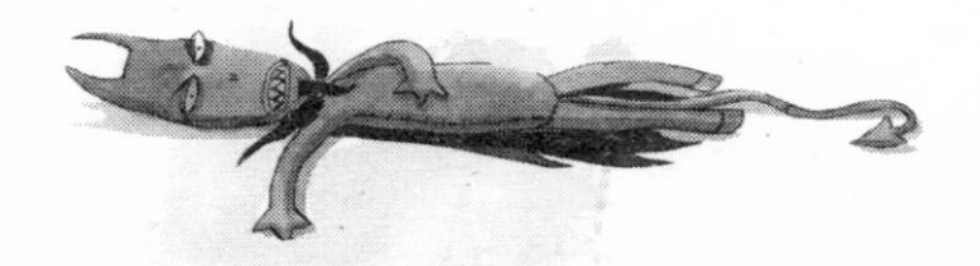

'Solstice,' said Solstice.

'Are you trying to make fun of me?' Brandish asked.

Solstice hung her head in her hands and sighed.

She turned to Cudweed.

'It's just as well you left Fellah in your room,' she said.

Sadly for her, Brandish heard this remark.

'Fellah? And what on earth is a Fellah?'

Cudweed's voice trembled as he answered.

'He's . . . he's . . . he's my monkey.'

Well, I won't tell you exactly how Mr Brandish reacted, but I think it would be fair to summarise the situation by saying that children and teacher had not got off to a great start.

It is also fair to say that I heard one or two words I haven't heard in a good long while, probably not since the Otherhands laid siege to the castle when it was owned by the Deffreeques. There was some choice language then, I can tell you, but you try keeping a civil tongue when someone pours boiling oil on you.

I sat through the whole tortuous morning, wondering what, if anything, I could do to save the children from their dreadful fate, until finally it was lunchtime and the gong summoned everyone to the Dining Hall.

'Very well, you may go,' Brandish said. 'After lunch, we will begin our studies of the Belgian legal system.'

Solstice and Cudweed practically ran from the room. I flung myself after them, and landed on Solstice's shoulder.

'Oh, Edgar,' she said, as I alighted. 'Are we glad to see you! Edgar, it's just terrible.'

Cudweed could barely speak, but nodded glumly in agreement.

Solstice looked up and down the corridor, then turned to Cudweed and me, and whispered, firmly and fiercely.

'He's got to go.'

Six

Minty's spells didn't always work too well. For example, there was the time one of her potions led to an outbreak of Frog Disease spreading throughout the castle. Much hopping followed.

Speaking of the monkey, the appallingly primitive primate known as Fellah, if I had had more of my bird brains about me, I might have realised that something was not normal. The monkey was not himself when he was present, though in fact, he was not present much of the time, but again I failed utterly to connect what needed connecting until it was very late in the day.

In my defence, I can only say that things were very confusing. There was much going on, and things were getting odder by the minute.

Over lunch we were treated to a display of knitted eyebrows from Lord Otherhand, which was a sign that he was thinking, and thinking hard. He had spent the morning working on concepts and designs for his 'Predictometer' as he had

started calling it, before it was even built.

But from the mopey expression on Flinch's face as he stood by the door, I suspected it was not going well. Once or twice, Valevine would open his mouth to say something, then shut it again, whereupon Minty told him it looked like he was trying to catch flies. A remark that he ignored.

She turned her attention instead to Solstice and Cudweed.

'So, children,' she said brightly. 'How is your new teacher settling in?'

Cudweed groaned as though he'd been shot, Solstice stared into her soup and stirred it wordlessly.

'Well? Children?'

Solstice flung her spoon down.

'He's awful!' she cried.

'Solstice! Come now. You can't say that about someone you've only just met.'

Why not? thought I, from a perch by the fireplace.

'But he is awful,' she protested.

Cudweed nodded furiously.

'He's mean. And nasty,' he said.

'And hairy. And short.'

'And he smells funny too. Like a wet dog.'

'And he's standing in the doorway,' said Valevine, and the children turned to see that their

father spoke the truth.

'Oh. No,' said Solstice, and her face fell so far it nearly ended up in her bowl.

'Now we're for it,' Cudweed whispered.

'I wonder,' said Brandish, coming into the dining hall, 'if I might trouble you for a dish of water?'

'A dish?' said Minty.

'Did I say a dish?' he replied. 'I mean, of course, a glass.'

Flinch went to oblige the short and hairy one and while he waited, Brandish stared at the children with loathing and hatred.

'So,' Minty ventured optimistically. 'Have you been a teacher a long time?'

'Yes,' said Brandish, and promptly shut his mouth again so he could resume glaring at his pupils.

Flinch returned with a glass of water and Brandish took it and stalked away.

'Remember, children,' he said over his shoulder as he went. 'The Belgian legal system awaits you after lunch.'

He left.

'See!' exclaimed Solstice. 'Mother, do you see?'

'What, dear? It sounds . . . fun.'

'Fun! Mother! He's trying to kill us with boredom!'

'That's enough now, dear. Can't you see your father is struggling to hear himself think?'

But Valevine at that moment stood up, waggling a finger in the air.

'Aha!' he cried. 'I have it!'

All so well and good. Though what was less good was that just at that moment, Fellah suddenly appeared as if from nowhere, jumped onto the table, landed on Solstice's discarded spoon and catapulted a glob of thick pea soup

right onto Lord Otherhand's forehead.

He showed remarkable dignity as he addressed Cudweed while green stuff dripped down his face.

'One day, that monkey will have to go,' he said, and began wiping with his napkin.

Cudweed was about to protest, but Solstice shot him a warning look.

'Not now,' she whispered.

'But it was just an accident,' Cudweed said. 'Just bad luck that Father stood up at that exact moment.'

Yes, I thought. Bad luck, old boy.

Bad luck.

And still my tiny old noggin did not manage to grasp what was going on in Castle Otherhand.

Seven

Solstice's favourite band are a hardcore death-gloom-thrash-trance-freak-out unit called I Was Born Wrong.

Oooooh!

The life of the raven is a strange one, that's for certain. Things had reached new levels of strange around the castle.

For example, on the second day of the children's schooling, there was a sudden spate of unusual accidents, resulting in the loss of three maids. The most bizarre was a freak accident with a cheese slicer which led to the demise of a pretty young parlour maid called Chloë.

As the fifth corpse in two days was carried out of the kitchen door by Box and Sons, Minty shook her head slowly.

'Something most unusual is occurring and I cannot conceive of what it is.'

Well, I agreed with that.

But if we thought things were weird then, it was as nothing to what lay in store.

Just before bedtime, I sat with Solstice and Cudweed over a glass of warm milk and honey and Cook's best biscuits, the ones with squashed flies in them, or raisins, if no flies could be found, which was usually the case. Solstice was idly playing Clock Patience with a beautiful set of cards, whereas Cudweed devoted his entire attention to the biscuits.

They had had another hard day of it.

'Edgar,' wailed Solstice. 'You have to help us! There has to be some way to get rid of him.'

'And quickly, too!' added Cudweed. 'Do you know what he had us do today?'

'Ark,' I said, which meant yes, I do, because I was sitting on the beam with my beak open in amazement at the new levels of boredom Brandish was capable of inflicting.

'We now know everything there is to know,' Solstice said, 'about coal mining in the Ukraine. And believe me, there's a lot to know.'

'Do you know?' Cudweed said suddenly. 'I've just realised. I'll never get that day back! Eight hours of my life wasted on drilling techniques! Just think what I could have been doing with eight hours! Sleeping! Eating! Playing with Fellah!'

'Where is your monkey, anyway?' Solstice asked.

Cudweed looked miserable. He picked up Solstice's pack of cards.

'I don't know. He's about somewhere, but he's not himself. He comes and goes, but he doesn't seem right.'

Well, I hate to appear mean, but that was good news for this old bird, at least, because a well monkey would be one that was chasing my tail feathers round the castle trying to strangle me.

Cudweed shuffled the cards and began flicking them across the table one by one.

'Did you hear about the three maids today?' Solstice asked Cudweed. 'That's a lot for one day. Even for us. Something strange is going on in this place.'

'**Arruk!**' I said, trying to agree, while

also pointing out that I could have told her that ages ago.

'Did you hear that they found a flock of sheep in the ballroom this afternoon? No one knows how they got in! And they were all wearing pink ribbons in their hair. Odd. Took ages to shoo them out into the pasture.'

'Coo,' said Cudweed.

'I know, but then I suppose sheep do odd things sometimes.'

'No, I mean, coo – look at the cards.'

He pointed to the pile of cards which

he'd been flicking. Each one had turned over as it went, and what we saw was every red card in the pack face up. Cudweed flicked through the cards left in his hand.

'All black . . .'

'So?' said Solstice. 'That's rather tasteful, isn't it? All black.'

'So, you saw me shuffle them first, didn't you?'

Solstice said nothing for a second, then she scratched her head.

'Gasp. Do you know what the odds against that are?'

'No, I don't and I don't want to because it sounds dangerously like you're trying to get me to do maths and we have maths all day tomorrow

with Mr Smelly.'

'Fair enough,' said Solstice, 'but let's just say it's very unlikely. Hmm. Why don't you do it again?'

Cudweed grabbed the cards back and gave them the biggest shuffle he could, largely by dropping them all on the floor first.

'Ready?' he said at last.

'Ready.'

Again he flicked the cards across the table, but this time they did not all come up red first. What they did was come up all black, until he was left with just the red ones in his hand.

If I had had hairs on the back of my neck, they would have stood up. As it was, I felt my feathers prickle and itch, and not just from fleas.

'That's just too, too weird,' said Solstice.

'Something, but something, is going on in this place.'

If anyone says that again, I thought, I will scream, pack my bags, and leave this castle for good. Yes, something weird is going on! But what?

The children went to bed, Cudweed still ruffling the cards between his fingers, as if they would reveal their secret to him.

I obligingly let myself be shut in my cage, and even decided I might spent the night there for once, just because I was so tired from all the thinking, and all the oddness.

I mean, the chances of a fatal accident while polishing melons must be so slim, but that was exactly what had happened to a maid called Jemima that morning,

And it was from the safety of my cage

that I witnessed something very peculiar indeed.

I think I'd been sleeping for a wee-bitty while, when all of a sudden I was wide awake, my super-senses leaping into full alertness, and I craned my head about, looking for the source of the problem.

Aaaah!

What I saw was the back end of a large, and I mean large, wolf, loping out of the Red Room, as proud as you please. And this too was peculiar, because there are absolutely no wolves allowed in the castle; not since that business with the vicar's children a few years back. The mess was awful.

I think that was when I finally realised that another mystery had descended upon Castle Otherhand, and that, once more, it would fall on me to save the day.

So be it! Edgar to the rescue!

But no point in not getting a good night's sleep first, I thought, so I shut my eyes and soon nodded off.

Eight

Edgar's claws need filing on a regular basis, or they can play havoc with the castle's soft furnishings, curtains, carpets, and cushions. And Minty's hairdo.

'Look!'

The following morning I knew I had not been hallucinating the wolf.

After breakfast, Solstice and Cudweed were on their way to the day of maths, when the bright girl stopped dead. She pointed at the floor.

'Footprints! And they are not human! Gasp!'

Cudweed came closer, and with his extraordinary knowledge of the animal kingdom, made an announcement.

'They belong to a dog,' he said.

'But they're so big!' Solstice said. 'It must be a very big dog.'

Futhork!

I screeched, which only brought a loud shhh from Solstice.

'Or . . .' inquired Cudweed. 'What are those very big dogs called?'

'Hounds?' suggested Solstice.

'Yes,' said Cudweed. 'No. Bigger than that.'

'Oh, you mean wolves.'

'Yes,' decided Cudweed. 'That's right. Bone-crunching, chop-slathering, hairy-howling wolves.'

'Ark!' I cried. At last. Thank you!

'Gasp!' said Solstice. 'You think there's a wolf on the loose? Eek! We must go and find Father and show him. He'll know what to do.'

Unlikely, I thought, but worth a go.

However, by the time that we'd found Lord Otherhand had already gone up to his inventing room and

would not be seen again all day, and then found Lady Otherhand, and returned to the corridor, the footprints had gone.

Vanished!

'Coo,' said Cudweed.

'Gasp!' said Solstice.

'Really, dears,' said Minty, sighing. 'I don't have time for your games today. I've got to speak to the agency about more maids. They're threatening to double the fees and you know how tight money is at the moment.'

'But, Mother!'

But Minty would not listen. I guess she's known the odd wolf or two in her younger days, if you know what I mean.

'And besides, you're already half an hour

late for school.'

Which was true, but strangely enough, the usually prompt Brandish was also late, for just then he came bustling down the corridor, herding the children into the classroom, and once more shutting the door on Minty and me.

'Nasty habit, that,' said Minty, and I nodded, hopping onto her shoulder.

'There's a nice bird,' she said. 'Do you know, Edgar, it feels like quite a while since we've had a proper chat. Probably not since that business with the kittens. Come on downstairs with me and you can cheer me up till the nasty agency people come. Honestly! You'd think we *meant* to kill their staff, the way they go on . . .'

And in this fashion, Minty and I descended

from the upper echelons of the castle and back down towards the lower levels.

As we went she told me how worried she was about money, and just what anyone thought they were going to do about it. All Valevine seemed to do was shut himself away trying to invent something that would make them all very rich, but sadly to date all his experiments had done was cost a fortune and endanger the lives of various servants and family members.

We came into the Great Hall, and were exactly underneath the huge crystal chandelier in the middle of the room when there was a terrible creaking noise and, a moment later, it was hurtling down towards us.

I shut my eyes, preparing for a quick, flat

and sparkly death, and Minty made a small squeaking noise.

The chandelier hit, and with an almighty crash and a deafening splintering of crystal dangly bits, we were killed.

Or at least, we should have been. After a second, I opened my eyes and realised that I could see and as far as I know, that shouldn't have been possible if I was dead.

Unless of course, I was a ghost.

I was woken from these thoughts by Minty, who assured me we were both still very much alive.

It seemed the chandelier had fallen all around us, just missing us on every side, leaving us totally unhurt.

'And you know,' she said quite calmly, 'there's been rather a bit too much of that sort of thing going on of late. Preposterously unlikely things happening. It rather reminds me of something, but I just can't think what . . .'

Well, I thought, I rather wish you would do some rapid thinking and work out what on earth is going on. Then we might be able to do something about it.

Hmm.

We passed through one of the smaller courtyards, underneath the East Tower, from the summit of which we could hear a frantic hammering and clattering. I decided to leave Minty to her appointment with the agency, and see what the old loony Lord was up to.

I nipped off Minty's shoulder and pointed my beak upwards, taking a few lazy turns around the courtyard and circling up to my favourite spot on the windowsill ledge outside Valevine's lab.

I tiptoed along and peered into the window.

Gasp.

That's what I would have said had I been Solstice.

Instead, I merely opened both eyes, and

beak, wide in amazement. For there, standing looking very like a finished piece of machinery, was the thing Lord Otherhand had been working on.

'Heh, heh!' Valevine was at that moment saying to Flinch, a disturbing habit he has picked up from Grandma S. 'Is this not a work of genius? Don't answer that, my man, just pass me that screwdriver, will you? The big one. No, bigger. No, the big one. Big!'

Flinch finally found the screwdriver of Valevine's dreams, and handed it to his Lordship, who began

banging on the side of the machine with it.

It was a funny-looking thing, but actually, I admit, it did almost look as though it might work.

It looked a little like a small piano, with an upright wooden case, some levers and knobs on a projection where the keyboard would have been, and then, a long slot along the front formed a narrow wooden window.

A moment or two later I realised it was in fact the practice piano from the Music Room, cruelly chopped about and recast in the new guise of Valevine's latest piece of lunacy.

'Heh,' repeated Valevine. 'Nearly there! And then we shall be ready to unveil the future, but right here and now. The vast unknowable sea of things yet to be will be known this very night! We shall have to concede that I am a genius of the greatest magnitude. Kings will bow before me with utter humility and total awe as they wonder what sort of man it is who can achieve such wonderful things!'

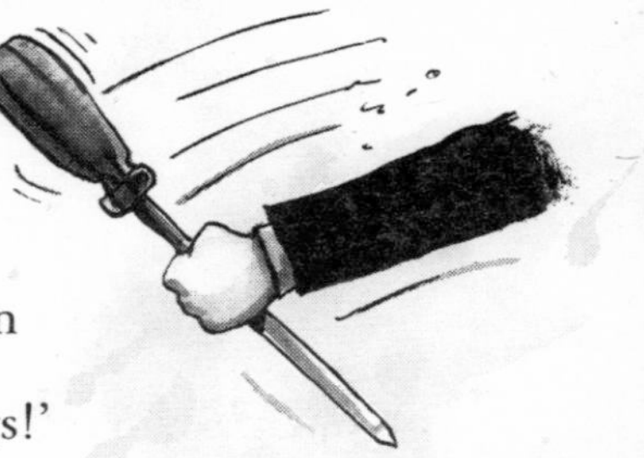

He whacked the top of the ex-piano a few more times, then stood back.

'Aha! What do you say, Flinch? Are we, as I believe the young people say these days, ready to rock?'

'Quite ready, sir,' said Flinch. 'More than ready.'

'Heh.'

Valevine stuck his chin out, and seemed to be addressing the wall as he gave an imaginary speech, in which he was presumably collecting a big shiny award, and a very large wodge of cash, too.

'Yes, that's right. Yes. No, not that hard, actually. Well, you know. Oh, of course, you'd like to see it work . . . Predict the future? Why yes, it's foolproof. Well, shall we give it a whirl? Oh no, it's very easy when you know how . . . Here, you merely dial in the date here. So. And then flick this switch, here. Gently! So! Ladies and Gentlemen, I give you . . . the Predictometer!'

At this point, I swear Flinch's eyes had rolled so far up that he was looking at the ceiling through the top of his skull, but finally Valevine wound a small handle on the side of the Predictometer, and flicked the switch he had spoken of.

The machine immediately began to rumble, and shake, like a washing machine at a disco. It began to shimmy across the floor towards the open doorway and certain doom down the spiral stairs, so Flinch and his Lordship had to rush across the room after it and restrain the thing.

As they pulled it back into place, I saw that the window slot across the front had gone crazy. Behind the slot, I could now see a series of barrels spinning at the highest velocity, so fast they were merely a blur.

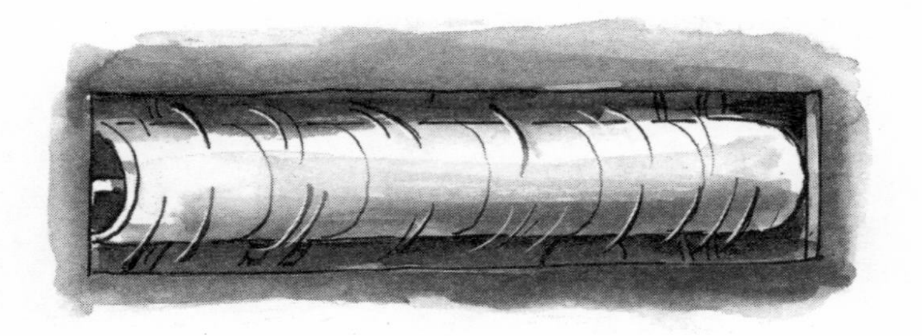

Suddenly, the first barrel, at the left, ground to a halt. It had a word on it.

The word was *butter*.

Before I had too much time to ponder

that, the second barrel stopped, and again, there was a word on it.

The second word was *monkeys*.

And then in rapid succession, as if the Predictometer was making up its mind, all the other barrels stuck into position.

It dawned on me that the machine had spelled out a sentence.

The sentence, if you can call it that, was:

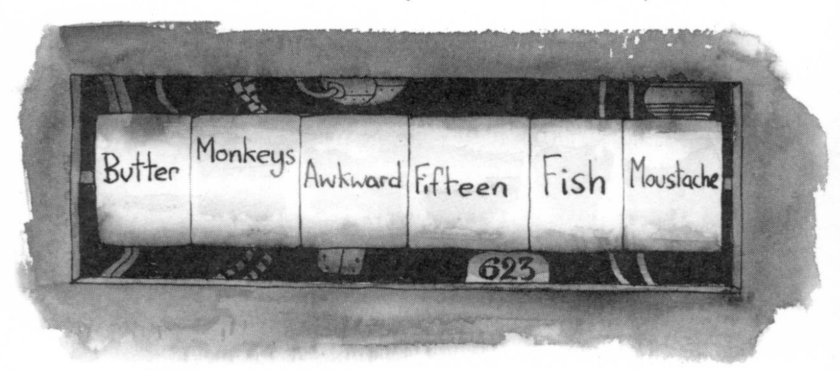

'Futhork!' I cried. Another disaster

for Valevine's inventing career, and for once, just for once, I actually thought he had been going to do something smart. I cursed myself for my stupidity, because I really had believed that the thing was going to work.

However, I seemed to be alone in that opinion.

'Flinch!' cried Valevine, staring excitedly at the words on the Predictometer. 'The future is revealed to us! Write that down! Heh!'

Flinch was already grabbing a pencil.

I fell backwards off the windowsill in alarm, and only remembered to flap my wings when I smelled the courtyard coming towards me at a dangerous speed.

Lunatics! I thought.

Lunatics and luck! A twin curse upon Castle Otherhand!

Nine

Solstice has a girly secret! Despite her solid goth credentials, she still has a favourite pink teddy bear, called Tiny Timothy.

'Do you know,' said Solstice at the end of the week, 'I've been thinking.'

I raised my head from a quick rootle for fleas that I hoped had gone unobserved by Solstice and Cudweed. I was in luck.

She was gazing out of her octagonal window, at the valley below.

Cudweed lay on the wolfskin rug, picking his way through a bowl of toffees. He always eats more when he's nervous. And he's nervous most of the time. He was slightly sulky because Cook had just announced that the intended Friday night dinner of a big fat roast was going to have

to be postponed because the beef had gone missing from the cold store.

In its place was a lentil casserole. Cudweed had barely spoken a word since hearing this.

'I've been thinking that no matter how much we tell Mother we don't want to be educated, and certainly not by Mr Hairy-and-Smelly, she will never listen to us. And there's no point even trying to talk to Father when he's in an inventing mood.'

Cudweed nodded, but still did not speak. He popped another toffee into his mouth because there's always the danger that the first one can run out just when you're not expecting it.

I hopped over to the windowsill by Solstice, in order to encourage her thoughts.

'I mean, have you seen Father's machine, Edgar?'

I had indeed, but Solstice had also now witnessed its fearsome fortune-telling powers. The previous evening, Valevine had called the whole family, and chief serving staff to a demonstration. He chose the yellow drawing room as the venue for this event, which was nice because it was a chilly evening and there's a lovely open fire in there.

Evening drew in as the guests assembled, even Grandma Slivinkov, I noticed. A log fire crackled in the grate, Flinch poured sherry for everyone, and Valevine stood by the machine, for

the moment hidden under a dust sheet. From time to time he would stick his head under the sheet and tamper with something, then come back out, smiling wordlessly at the assembled party.

There had then followed an even longer version of the speech he'd inflicted on Flinch at the moment of the machine's birth.

Finally he had whipped the dust sheet away, to an underwhelming gasp from the crowd.

At this point, Slivinkov seemed to wake up and leaned forward.

'Is that my old piano?' she asked, squinting at the Predictometer.

'Piano? How unlikely! Flinch, more sherry for Granny, I think.'

Valevine moved into a long and protracted explanation of precisely how clever he was, and at last, we were treated to the first *official* utterance of the Predictometer.

Wobble egg trombone blue square hippopotamus.

'Honestly,' said Solstice, still gazing out of her octagonal window, as she tried to remember what the machine had said. 'He set the machine to tell the future for next Friday, what did it say? "Elephant green potatoes wig tremendous piglets." Or something like that. I admit I might have forgotten. But Flinch wrote it down.'

He had indeed, and Valevine seemed genuinely hurt that no one could see the brilliance of his invention in quite the way he could. This hadn't stopped him from flicking the machine into life a few more times that evening, and among its more memorable utterances were:

Rounding noise balloon sausage fruit box.

After fish speak plummet bread penguin.

And my favourite of all:

Because water dancing smell jelly baboons.

'What are we going to do, Edgar? It seems we're on our own. And it seems that if we're going to get rid of Mr Brandish, then we need to give Mother and Father a really good reason why. He's plainly a nasty, mean, and evil weevil, so all we need to do is prove it. For one thing, have you noticed that he's still wearing the same clothes he arrived in? And that trunk of his was supposed to be full of them. He must be up to something, and we only need to find out what.'

She stopped, building up for her big idea.

Cudweed was paying attention now, waiting for her plan. Anything that could save him from another minute of trigonometry was worth listening to.

'What we need to do,' she said, 'is spy on him!'

'That's a bit naughty, isn't it?' Cudweed said at last. 'Even for us.'

'Come on, Cudweed, oh brother of mine. Be strong. We have to do it. If we can find something deeply unpleasant about him, they'll have to get rid of him, see?'

'Well,' said Cudweed. 'If you put it that way.'

'I do! And we have to act, because we're alone on this one, just you and me!'

Wait a minute. Alone?

'**Arruk!**' I squawked.

'Yay!' cried Solstice. 'We've got Edgar, too!'

Ten

Valevine cannot abide rock music. He hates it so much that even the single word 'guitar' is enough to send him into a blue funk for days.

Solstice is a smart girl, so I have to admit that I thought there might be more to her plan than there actually was. It was pretty basic stuff really, and it went like this:

1. Wait until bedtime, and then go to bed

2. (Which she thought was the really clever part) Only pretend to go to sleep, and then get up again

3. Sneak up to Brandish's room, and . . .

4. Peek through the keyhole.

I suppose you can say it had a certain beautiful simplicity to it.

Cudweed, however, still had some problems with the plan, chief of which was:

'Supposing we get caught?'

But Solstice would not be dissuaded, and

her only other thought on the matter was this:

'Cudweed, you may not bring Fellah on this adventure. He is too noisy and likely to get us more caught than otherwise.'

Strangely, Cudweed agreed to this.

'The trouble is, though, I don't even know where he is half the time these days. He's gone very odd indeed and when I do see him, he's a very glum monkey.'

'Hmm,' said Solstice. 'Well, I bet that whatever's going on in this castle has got something to do with his glumness. As soon as we sort it all out, he'll be right as rain, you'll see.'

Oh wonderful, I thought. I have another idea. Couldn't we just leave the monkey miserable and see how everyone gets on with that?

'Right! Off to bed! Then once Mother's done her patrol, give it half an hour and meet at the fifth floor landing. Yes?'

'Okay,' nodded Cudweed.

'Wait!' said Solstice. 'How are you going to stay awake? And how are you going to know when half an hour's gone?'

'Easy,' said Cudweed. 'I am going to eat forty-three toffees.'

'Have I missed something?'

'It takes me half an hour to eat forty-three toffees. Exactly.'

Solstice looked at her little brother, her head on one side. I think she gets it from me.

'I cannot decide if you are stupider, or smarter than you look.'

'Thanks,' said Cudweed, happy to take that as a compliment.

We went our separate ways, and with Nanny Lumber absent, presumably experimenting upon small animals somewhere on her conference, it was Lady Otherhand who did the evening lights out.

As soon as she'd gone, I wondered how *I* was going to stay awake and know when half an hour was up, but I needn't have worried, because I was still worrying when Solstice snuck into the Red Room to come and get me.

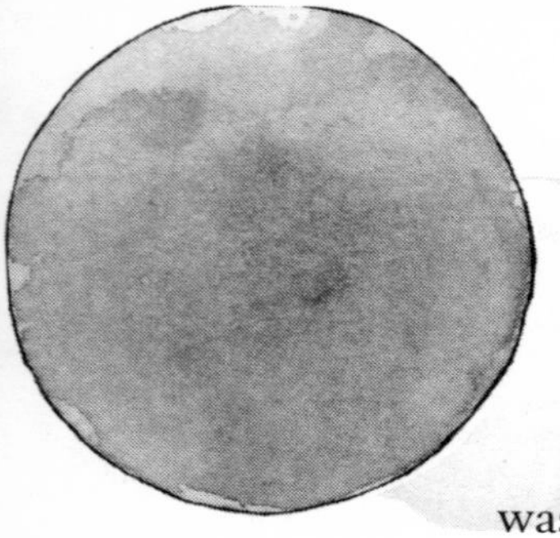

We found Cudweed already waiting for us on the fifth floor landing. It was a full moon, and there was plenty of moonlight to see by without the need for lamps.

'You're early,' said Solstice.

Cudweed shrugged.

'Must be getting better at eating toffees,' he said thoughtfully.

'Never mind,' whispered Solstice. 'Here we go.'

And there we went, making our way up to the room allocated to Mr Melvin Brandish.

Once there, Solstice shoved Cudweed forward.

'You go first,' she whispered. 'Have a look!'

'Why me?' whimpered Cudweed too loudly.

'Shh!' hissed Solstice. 'Because he might be, you know, getting undressed or something, and I'm a lady and ladies shouldn't see such things.'

'I'm not sure I want to either,' said Cudweed, but Solstice pushed him towards the keyhole.

'Go on! What's he doing? Is he there?'

Cudweed jumped back from the keyhole as if he'd been bitten on the nose.

'Coo!' he said. 'In fact, gasp! Have a look, Solstice. He's not in there, but . . . but . . . but there's a . . . a wolf in there! A wolf!'

'Nonsense,' said Solstice, but was soon dragging Cudweed out of the way to see for herself.

She had a good long look, and then, still peering through the hole, said,

'Well, I admit he's a bit hairier than a person ought to be, but really I think you're exaggerating slightly, Cudweed.'

'What do you mean?' stammered

Cudweed, scratching his nose.

'I mean, have a look. He's in there, and I know it's not pleasant when he's only wearing his underpants, but he's quite clearly him, and there's no wolf to be seen, so I can only assume you're losing it slightly.'

Cudweed bent to the keyhole again, and saw what Solstice had seen.

'Blimey,' he said. 'Are people supposed to be that hairy? But listen, I saw a wolf in there, I'm telling you. A wolf.'

Solstice pulled Cudweed away again.

'Never mind that. We just need to catch him doing . . .'

Now Solstice shrieked, and fell back from the keyhole.

'Gasp!' she cried. There was a noise of the key scrabbling in the lock on the other side of the door.

Rumbled!

'Run,' cried Solstice. 'Run for your lives!'

And so we did, although I decided that Solstice probably wouldn't mind if I flew instead, because ravens are really bad at running, and it looks totally stupid too.

Eleven

Solstice and Cudweed have three cousins, whom they detest. Their names are Tiffany, Jasper, and Cynthia, and all three are vile. Even Minty, whose sister they belong to, has been known to say, rather gruesomely, that they should have been 'taken to the river'.

There was much thinkery and ponderment after the incident at the keyhole.

Cudweed, Solstice and I retired to do some mulling on top of the brain-scratching, and Cudweed decided that it would be best to do this over a cup of hot chocolate and some sugar mice. Personally I would have preferred the real thing, but I did get my beak fairly stuck into one of the little white sweets and found it to be acceptable food for thought.

It had been a panicky job, the whole fleeing thing, and no one looked twice to see what awful beast was coming after us down the hall.

The children skidded round the corner of the corridor as though they were on jet-propelled ice skates, and I flapped so hard I was in severe danger of my wings coming off. In this way we made a noisy retreat as we fled the scene, and, high-tailing it to the kitchens for company and safety, we arrived in a fluster.

Cook seemed to sense the seriousness of the situation. Cudweed called for refreshments, and we paused to consider what we'd seen.

The thinking, and the conversation, went like this:

'What did you see?'

'I don't know. What did you see?'

'Well, I saw Brandish one minute.'

'And then a wolf the next?'

'Yes! A wolf! Gasp! The bone-crunching and chop-slathering sort.'

'What can it mean?'

'Well, think about it.'

Solstice stood up, and drained the dregs of her hot chocolate.

'Did you notice the moon tonight, Cudweed?'

Cudweed shivered a bit.

'No. Was it . . . ?'

'Yes! A full moon! What does that make you think of?'

He made a tiny whimpering sound, which Solstice seized upon.

'Aha! You think it too!'

'No,' Cudweed protested. 'I'm not thinking

anything about anything!'

'Yes you are!' cried the gloomiest girl in the county. 'Yes. And think how hairy he is! And how smelly! And the paw prints in the hallway, and him being late for school, and the full moon, and the missing leg of beef from the kitchens, and then one minute he's him and the next minute . . . the next minute . . . he's a . . . come on, Cudweed, you know what I'm getting at! He's . . .'

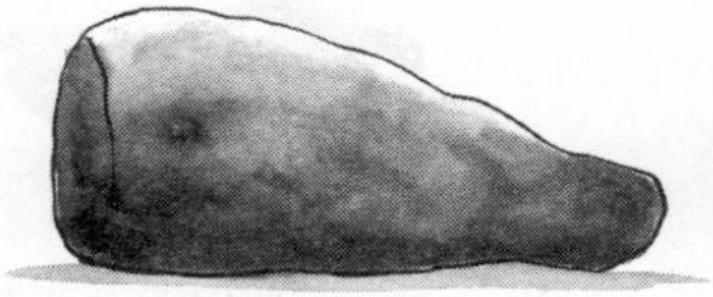

'. . . a wolf,' said Cudweed, in a very unhappy voice.

'Exactly!' declared Solstice, helping herself to another sugar mouse.

Cudweed sniffed and, with some icing

sugar giving him a white moustache, he looked extremely pathetic.

'He's a werewolf, isn't he?'

'I very much fear that he is!' said Solstice, sounding rather unfeared of the whole rotten business. 'And,' she added, 'we are going to have to prove it to our recalcitrant relatives!'

Cudweed frowned.

'Our prevaricating parents.'

Cudweed's frown got worse.

'Mother and Father,' Solstice explained patiently. 'Because they're really dim sometimes.'

Cudweed nodded.

'You know what, though?' he asked.

'What's that, brother dear?'

'I didn't know that werewolves actually existed. I thought that they were, you know, made up. And stuff.'

'Hmm,' said Solstice. 'Maybe. But if there's even the smallest chance that they do exist, then I think you would have to agree that what we witnessed with our own eyes in this very castle this very day would have to be a certain and proven case of a werewolf, yes?'

I think Cudweed was slightly lost by now, but he got the gist of what she was saying, which was basically that if anyone anywhere had ever seen a werewolf, then what we had seen was certainly one.

'And,' she continued, 'if that is the case, then we can only say what a highly unusual occurrence it would be. And in that case, I would just like to say one thing. Namely that this whole castle is just one weird thing after another at the moment!'

'Arkk!' I screeched. She was dead right, if I may slip into slang for a moment, and as if to prove her point, Fellah the monkey sauntered into the kitchens wearing a tiny little white wedding dress, and smoking a pipe.

He didn't look too sure about either.

Twelve

Edgar's an old raven, and it takes special care to keep him ship-shape and trim. His favourite beak polish is called Flunkett's Shinewell, and he won't accept anything else.

I think now might be a good time for a word about monkeys.

Aaark!

I don't know if you've been following me at all, but if you have, I think there's a chance that you might have picked up on the fact that I have, how shall I put it . . . a very bad opinion of monkeys.

I mean, to put it plainly, what are monkeys *for?* Really?

It's a question I suspect you will struggle to answer because I have wrestled with it myself ever since the arrival of Fellah at Castle Otherhand, and I have found no satisfactory answer.

Are they useful? No.

Do they look nice? Definitely not.

Do they sound nice? They do not.

Do they smell nice? Quite the opposite!

And furthermore, if the pickle-brained specimen we have to live with is anything to go by, they seem to be masters at being loud, irritating, smelly, ugly and rude.

What's that? What's that you say?

You say, that from a monkey's point of view, perhaps ravens are pointless, ugly and irritating. Well, I've considered that too, and I have only this to say – **futhork!**

I hope that clears things up for you.

And anyway, don't change the subject, it's monkeys we're talking about here. Where was I?

Yes! Pointless, irritating, rude, smelly, dumb, stupid and limited, noisy, smelly, aggressive, ugly, hairy and smelly. Did I mention that? The stink?

The unholy aroma! The noxious reek! The manksome odour! The simply unbelievable pong!

Though truth to say, it is perhaps the one feature of Fellah that is of some use to me, because it has on numerous occasions acted as an early warning system of the presence of the murderous monkey only an arm's grab behind me, and closing. Such is the strength of his niffiness, and it has allowed me to take to the air in good time to avoid thin monkey fingers throttling me unawares.

Since Fellah arrived in the castle, not a day has gone by without some riotous nonsense occurring, some disturbance of the natural order, and some mess on the carpet somewhere or other.

And neither has a day gone by without a concerted and desperate attempt on my life by the brainless beast, or at least, it hadn't, until this recent business.

Ever since the day of the earthquake, I have to admit, Fellah has not been himself.

That much was clear, but as Cudweed gently took the pipe from Fellah's paws, and Solstice helped him out of the wedding dress, I think we were all thinking the same thing. Namely, that Fellah had reached his most bizarre activity yet.

Something nagged at my thoughts, like a mouse in a frayed jumper, tugging away, but not getting out. It had all started on the day of the earthquake, and in some way Fellah was connected to it all. For the life of me I could not get my thoughts to sit straight and behave in my brain.

'What is going on in this place?' Cudweeed enquired of his sister.

'Put that pipe out, there's a good brother,' said Solstice, neatly folding the dress into four. 'And where on earth did this come from?' she added.

Cudweed shrugged.

'The same place as that delivery of square footballs yesterday?'

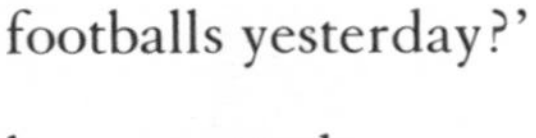

he suggested.

'Just think.

Where would we have put forty-two of them?'

'Hmm,' said Solstice, pondering. 'I don't think I know.'

'**Arrk!**' I cried.

'Yes,' agreed Solstice. 'Yes, Edgar, it is all jolly strange.'

Fellah sat on the carpet, his silly feet pointing up, and his spindly legs sticking straight out. His head dropped on his chest, and altogether he looked like a defeated chimp. A beaten monkey, sad and forlorn.

I almost felt sorry for him.

But only almost.

'Oh! Solstice!' Cudweed howled. 'What are we going to do?'

She shook her head.

'I don't know. But an even more worrisome thought has just arrived in my head. In fact, now I come to think of it, gasp!'

Cudweed's bottom lip stuck out a bit and began to tremble.

'What . . . what is it?' he asked, dreading the answer.

'Simply this. We are being taught by a werewolf! We may have fled from the scene of his hairiness upstairs, but tomorrow morning we shall have to report to class, and there and then, we will be taught by a werewolf. Just think! At any moment, he could transform before our eyes into that oversized carnivorous canine, and gobble us both up before we'd even handed in our French homework!'

Cudweed shuddered, and fell silent.

'Although . . .' Solstice said, suddenly brightening a little. 'Although, it might be that, actually, we're safe for the time being.'

'How's that?' Cudweed asked.

'Well, the moon of course! We saw him become a werewolf at the full moon, did we not? Which was last night. So if he's a normal type of werewolf, that means he won't become hairy again for another month.'

'Yes,' said Cudweed, perking up nicely.

But then his face fell again. 'So what you're saying is, we've got a month to live. And then we're dog food.'

'Yes,' said Solstice. 'No. What I'm saying is, we've got a month to get rid of him.'

Cudweed said nothing. He didn't look too happy about anything.

'Don't worry,' said Solstice soothingly. 'I have a plan.'

Thirteen

Although Cudweed is officially a scaredy-cat, he does feel a bit braver when he prowls the battlements with his crackshot catapult, known affectionately as Splatter-Skull.

Taught by a werewolf!

It wasn't a pretty thought.

And I, the feathered friend of all good people of Castle Otherhand, was the only line of defence for poor Solstice and Cudweed. They had long ago given up any notion that they might be able to make their parents,

a) Take any interest in them whatsoever, let alone . . .

b) Believe them when they tried to tell them their teacher was a werewolf, despite all the evidence to that end.

With trembling hearts therefore, all three of us set off for class the following morning, Solstice and Cudweed taking the conventional route into the room by the door, and I by my hidden path to the beam above Brandish's head.

The mood was tense, and I could see Cudweed's glasses steaming up with fear already.

Brandish was occupying himself at his desk, making a great show of leafing through the children's homework from the day before. He made several loud tutting noises, then sighed with heavy and dramatic sarcasm. Then he went back to flicking through the papers. Solstice was staring hard at Brandish, presumably looking for evidence of wolfishness;

bristling eyebrows, hairy hands, and yellow eyes, and I have to be honest and say that Brandish had all of these things, and a few more besides.

Cudweed, however, was by now shaking so hard that I thought his glasses might fall off.

I remembered what Solstice had told her little brother before class.

'Now listen,' she said, firmly but kindly. 'It's very important that we don't let Mr Hairy know we're on to him. Got it? We need to pretend things are utterly normal, and that we have no idea that he's a werewolf. Okay? Then we can wait until a good time to put my plan into action. Yes?'

Cudweed had nodded.

But as I looked at him now, I wondered whether he would be able to hold it together for five minutes, never mind a whole morning.

Finally, Brandish stopped fiddling with his papers, and fixed Cudweed with a steely glare.

'So, boy,' he said. 'Chemistry . . . explain oxidisation to me, if you'd be so kind . . .'

Cudweed opened his mouth and a small noise came out.

The noise was, wuh.

'Wuh,' he said. 'Wuh, wuh, wuh.'

Solstice groaned and let her head sink forward on to the desk.

'Oh no,' she said quietly to the desktop.

'Wuh,' said Cudweed, and then could contain himself no more.

'Werewolf!' he yelled at the top of his voice, and, sending his desk flying, ran from the room screaming.

There was a long, long silence, which finally Brandish broke.

'Your brother . . . ?' he asked, arching a bristly brow at Solstice.

'Heh, heh,' she said, attempting a note of jollity. 'Silly boy, reading too many scary stories when he should be asleep. Not himself this morning. Take no notice. Does it all the time. Heh, heh. Oxidisation, you say? Oxidisation may be defined as the combination of a substance with oxygen, or more correctly, a reaction in which the atoms in an element lose electrons and the valence of the element is correspondingly increased. Why, sir? Are we doing chemistry today? I *love* chemistry . . .'

So Solstice went on for about half an hour, by the end of which time, Brandish seemed to have forgotten that Cudweed even existed, never mind that he'd run screaming from the room making wild accusations about hairiness.

Also by the end of this time, I think there's quite a large possibility that I had fallen asleep, obviously for only the briefest of moments, but I woke to find myself dribbling and almost toppling off my perch.

With joy I noted that my drool had at

least fallen on Brandish's shoulder, but decided it might be time to leave Solstice to it. If anything, I had started feeling sorry for her teacher by the time she got to explaining the difference between oxidisation and reduction.

I shuffled backwards into the hole from whence I had come, and decided to seek out the shrieking child known as Cudweed.

However, his was not the first nose I noted on my sally through the castle, for as I exited my secret passage to the classroom, I heard more yells and curses coming from a nearby corridor.

What skulduggery is this? I wondered, and turned beakwards to the commotion.

I flew this way and that, and soon found the problem: Lord Otherhand and the long-suffering

Flinch were attempting to move the Predictometer up a small and extremely spirally stairway.

'Dammit, man!' cried Valevine. 'Push! Push like the devil is at your back!'

Flinch gave a mighty heave and the Predictometer shifted another step and then came to a grinding halt again.

'Time for a rest, I think,' declared

Valevine, and then caught sight of me watching the performance.

'Ah, Edgar, my boy!' Valevine grinned at me. 'How's life in the world of birds? How's it, you know, working out for you? The whole raven thing. Eh?'

I ignored his nonsense, and decided to set myself on top of the ex-piano, the future-telling machine, but as I was about to do so, I noticed something very peculiar indeed.

What I noticed was this: I noted that the machine still bore its most recent ludicrous pronouncement which it must have chuntered out when Valevine last switched it on.

I say ludicrous, but I will leave you to judge for now, because the sentence was this:

And at that point, my tiny little heart started thumping like a gorilla in a cupboard, and my overworked brain started to spin like a goldfish in a tumble dryer.

Could it be, could it be, that the infernal machine had actually worked? Sort of?

Fourteen

Solstice's first words came when she was quite big, and having spent the first three years of her life watching everything, she then announced to the grown-ups at teatime one day, 'Don't any of you ever do anything sensible?'

As you know, I am quite the philosopher. Quite the thinker of deep and meaningful thoughts, and I like to feel that I can plummet to the depths of the well of any problem and emerge with a solution wriggling in my stylish beak.

And now, once again, I saw the chance to act to save the day! With a little hop in my heels, I fled the scene of the precariously-placed Predictometer and hunted down an ally, namely, Solstice.

I needed her to see what I had seen; the unwittingly accurate sentence on her father's latest contraption, and I needed her to see it before they either dropped the blasted thing down five flights of stairs, or indeed, used it again, and erased that message for ever!

There was no time to lose, and I found Solstice after school hours in the kitchens, holding a very large leg of lamb in her arms.

She jumped when she heard me flap up behind her, and, when she had recovered, looked very guilty.

'Look, Edgar,' she said. 'There's no need to tell anyone that you've found me with this, is there? It's all part of my plan and I need it to help get rid of Brandish, so you just keep it to yourself, like a good boy, yes?'

'**Arruk!**' I squawked.

‘Thanks, Edgar,’ she said. ‘You are a good, good bird, and I love you very much. But don’t go thinking it was me who stole the beef the other day, because it wasn’t? Brandish must have polished that off for a snack one morning . . . quick! Someone’s coming!’

She was right. Footsteps were approaching, most likely Cook’s, and, though it was late in the day, the castle was by no means asleep.

Solstice fled the scene as fast as she could holding a leg of a sheep that was half her height, and I kept watch ahead and behind as she made her way back to her room.

In all the excitement, I had forgotten all about getting Solstice’s help.

Now that the lamb was safely stowed

under her bed, and she pulled the black velvet bedspread down to hide it, I began to tug like a loony at the hem of her long dress.

'Edgar! Get off! What are you doing?'

I kept pulling.

'Edgar! Really! What *has* got into you? Stop it!'

I didn't.

'Edgar! Are you feeling all right? Do you want something?'

I stopped and cried, **'Aark!'** and then I think she got it.

I sped out of the door with no more explanation and I knew it had worked when I heard her calling after me along the corridor.

'Edgar! Wait! Are you feeling okay? Is

this like that time with the walrus?'

And so on.

I did not stop, and I was soon on the steps to the East Tower, heading for Valevine's sacred laboratory at the top.

Solstice was growing alarmed now, but I was not to be dissuaded.

With alarm of my own I saw that Flinch, Valevine and the Predictometer had all left the spot in which I last saw them. So I hurtled on, and burst into Lord Otherhand's inventing space through the half open door.

Valevine harrumphed loudly upon seeing me, but when Solstice followed me into the room, all hell broke out.

'Solstice!' Valevine roared. 'What are you

doing in here? Get that blasted bird out of this room at once! This is a controlled environment! Any foreign body can cause great disturbance to my works!'

And so on.

I ignored him, and began tugging at Solstice's dress again, pulling her over to the Predictometer, to see what I had read there.

But Solstice was busy apologising to her father and trying to grab at my wings at the same time, and then! Disaster! I saw that they had already used the machine again, and instead it bore a new legend.

Blow hairy tube sheep suck mumbles.

I sank in a feathery heap of despair onto the flags of the lab floor feeling a little sorry for myself.

Noticing I had deflated somewhat, Solstice scooped me up and seemed very concerned.

'What is it, Edgar?' she said.

How could I explain? All my efforts wasted, and now just another piece of random nonsense on the dratted machine.

'Come on, Edgar. I think Father would like us to leave. Come on, I'll find you something horrible to eat. You'd like that, wouldn't you?'

As so, we were just leaving the room, when I heard Valevine say something most interesting.

'Write that one down, Flinch, and then we'll give the old girl another bash, eh?'

Of course!

Leaping from Solstice's clutches, I saw the very thing I was after, a single slip of paper among many, and plucking it between upper and lower beak, I flew from the room, to more shouts and curses from Lord Otherhand.

'One day,' he said, as I departed, 'that bird will have to go!'

But I didn't care, because once safely out of harm's way, I slowed to a cruising glide, and let Solstice catch up with me.

'What's the great mystery?' she said, taking the paper from my grasp. She read it herself, and her mouth fell open.

'This was one of the machine's things?'

she asked. 'An utterance of the Predictometer, that Flinch wrote down?'

'Ark!' I cried, and then added.

'Caw!'

She read aloud.

'Smoking white monkey dress pipe stupid.'

For a moment she was speechless, and then she found the only word she could at that precise moment.

'Gasp.'

Fifteen
Flinch rarely gets
a day off, being
overworked by
Lord Valevine in a
most terrible way.
However, when he
gets the chance he
does enjoy baking
fairy cakes, pink
and yellow ones
in particular.

There are moments in a raven's career when he wonders what he does it all for, why he bothers, who the hoot cares and so on, and this turned out to be one of those moments. For no sooner had I thought I had Solstice's attention and, therefore, her assistance, than I realised I had lost it again.

'Yes,' she said. 'Gasp. Very interesting. Now, back to work!'

'Ark-Ark?' I crowed, puzzled.

Solstice set off towards her room, and I had no choice but to follow.

'Raaark!' I tried to insist, but she was having none of it.

'Well, I admit it's quite interesting that Father has invented something that seems to have worked, but I have other geese to pluck.

And I mean, this is only one sentence, just one, that maybe accidentally came true.'

Accidentally?

Smoking white monkey dress pipe stupid.

The probability it was right by accident seemed even more unlikely than the probability of Valevine inventing something that worked. Even the slowest human could see that a quick rearrangement of the words would give you: stupid monkey, white dress, smoking pipe.

What more proof could you need?

But Solstice was not convinced.

'What about all the other things it's said?' she asked. 'What about "Rounding noise balloon sausage fruit box" or "After fish speak plummet bread penguin"? Hey? When are we going to see those come true?'

She had a point.

She flounced around a corner and was back at her bedroom door.

At that moment, the door to Cudweed's room opened, and he shuffled out looking glummer than ever.

'Seen my monkey?' he said, but there was little hope in his voice.

'Sorry,' said Solstice. 'Now, it's time for me to get on with my plan. I call it 'The Wolf Trap', and it's really rather amazing. What's going to happen is . . .'

'Futhork!' I cried, so loud that I stopped Solstice in her tracks. If she wasn't interested in uncovering the deeper mysteries of

Castle Wackiness, my only chance was her brother. I snatched the slip of paper about monkeys back from her, and deposited it on Cudweed's head.

'Hey, Edgar! Stop messing around.'

'I think he wants you to read it,' Solstice explained. 'It seems Father might have actually made something that works . . .'

Cudweed read the note.

Then he read it again.

And then he read it again.

And then he almost shouted, 'This means Fellah, doesn't it?'

Smart boy, I thought. Slow, but he gets there in the end.

'Yes, but I don't have time to waste,'

Solstice sighed. 'If we're going to get rid of Brandish, I have LOTS of work to do.'

Cudweed thought about it for a minute. He seemed to be trying to make up his mind about something. His mouth opened and closed a couple of times.

Then he said, very quietly, 'Don't you think we should let Father know about this?'

I took the opportunity, and went berserk, losing a few wing-tip feathers in the process. I almost chipped my beak on the ceiling.

Solstice sighed very heavily.

'Sigh!' she said, and then looked Cudweed straight in the eye.

'Very well. If you two think it's that important, you go and try and explain it to Father.

Personally, having just raided his laboratory and being made very unwelcome, I'm going to stay clear for a while. And someone has to expose Brandish as a hairy beastie. So! We'll divide our forces . . . if only to keep Edgar happy.'

Really! Keep *me* happy? And there's me thinking I was trying to save the castle. And everyone in it.

Again!

'Now,' said Solstice. 'I need a screwdriver, a hammer, a long coil of rope. And that leg of lamb.'

And off she went, humming a happily gloomy tune.

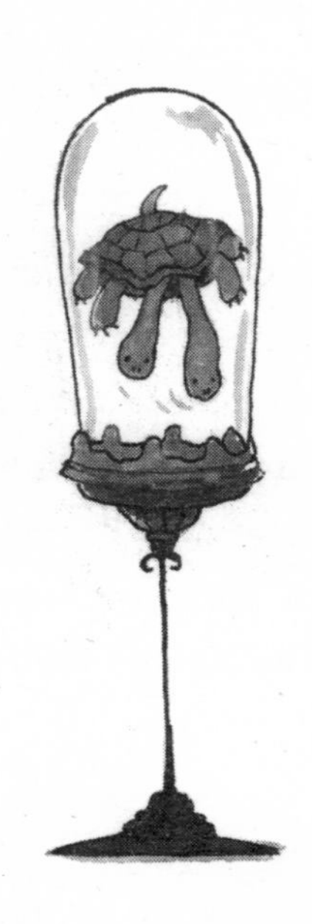

Sixteen

Cudweed was a strange baby and learned to talk very early, though his first words were, for some reason, all the names of food.

Night was falling as Cudweed and I made our way back through the castle once more, heading for the lab at the top of the East Tower, illuminated by a few silvery stars in the heavens.

Cudweed's nerve was failing him already.

'Supposing,' he said, which is, to tell the truth, a word that Cudweed often selects to begin sentences with. 'Supposing that Father is very unhappy to see us? Supposing he's, you know, cross? Something like that. What then, Edgar?'

I hopped onto Cudweed's shoulder.

'**Ark**,' I said, reassuringly. It was always a possibility, but it was one we had to face.

We walked on a few more steps, and then Cudweed stopped again.

'Supposing,' he said, 'that we can't make

him listen to us, and I get sent to bed without any supper, and you get locked in your cage for a week? Supposing that?'

'Kawk!' I said, a little more firmly. Come on now, boy, I thought, don't let me down just yet. All we have to do is show that piece of paper to your strange father and we're home and dry. Sort of.

'And supposing,' Cudweed said, 'that we really ought to be helping Solstice instead, and because we don't help her she gets caught by Brandish as she's setting up whatever her trap is? Have you thought about that, Edgar? Have you? I wouldn't want to be the one to let her get eaten. Would you?'

Now, I almost caved in myself, because,

damn and blast it all, he was right. I'm fond of Solstice, very fond, and the thought of anything bad happening to her was not a pleasant one to contemplate.

'But then, supposing we don't tell Father, and he never knows that his machine is working, and that impending doom impends on us all and that's the end of the castle and everyone in it because we didn't see it coming? Supposing that?'

Futhork! I had had enough. I dropped off Cudweed's shoulder and pecked his backside. Hard.

'Ow!' he said, but stayed standing where he was. So I did it again.

'Even more ow!' he cried, and hopped forward. Now I had him! And I pecked him so

hard he ran off down the corridor and up the stairs to Lord Otherhand's lab, with me giving him the odd jab in the rear end just in case he started saying 'supposing' again.

So it was for the second time in an hour that bird and child burst into the secret, sacred and most inner sanctum of Lord Valevine of Castle Otherhand.

What we found was Flinch and Valevine, both sitting in easy leather armchairs, feet up on the lab tables, each sporting a big spoon in one

hand and very large bowl of chocolate ice cream in the other.

'And that,' Valevine was saying casually, 'is why the sausage is better than the bicycle . . .'

But he stopped saying that very quickly, and started saying something else instead, in fact, he started shouting.

'Whaaaaat? I thought I told you that blasted bird was never allowed back in this room! Cudweed! What are you doing, boy?'

Cudweed skidded into room, came to a standstill, and then seeing his father looming at him waving a fairly hefty spanner, set off around the room again, at a steady trot.

'Father,' he panted, over his shoulder as he went. 'Wait! Father! Wait!'

'No, boy,' Valevine declared. 'You just wait! Wait till I get my hands on you! Flinch! Catch the bird!'

Well, there was no chance of that happening. I hopped onto a high beam, well out of reach of even the tallest and jumpiest butler, and watched as Flinch reluctantly got to his feet, and with a last lick of his spoon, went to fetch a step ladder from the corner of the room.

'Wait!' cried Cudweed, even more desperately. 'Wait!'

He was slowing up now, but fortunately for him, so was his father.

They ran round and around, until finally they were no more than walking.

'Just . . .' panted Valevine. 'Just . . . ahem . . . wait . . .'

'Wuh,' said Cudweed, still a pace ahead of his exhausted father. 'Wait a moment. Read . . .'

And he waved the slip of paper in Valevine's face, who came to a complete stop, and took the note.

'What's this?' he said.

'Your . . . machine . . .' said Cudweed.

'Yes?'

'Said that.'

'And?'

'Came true,' gasped Cudweed, and flumped onto the floor.

Flinch stopped trying to climb the ladder towards me and returned to ground.

'May I, Lordship?' he said and inspected the piece of paper. 'Yes,' he decided. 'Definitely one of ours.'

Valevine's face began to twitch, in all sorts of interesting ways.

'Came . . . true,' he panted, 'you say?'

Cudweed had nearly passed out, and his face was the colour of a pulped pomegranate.

'Uh-huh,' he said, heedless of the effect that slang might have on his father at such a critical moment. 'Fellah came into my room. Wearing little white dress. Smoking . . . pipe.'

'Really,' said Valevine thoughtfully, then, 'Really?'

'Really. Of course the bit about him being stupid isn't true.'

'Rarak!' I said from on high.

'Quite so, Edgar,' said Valevine. 'Quite. Cudweed . . . you have done well, my boy. Very well. Do you hear, Flinch? It seems that I have achieved a greatness the like of which most mortals can only dream. Can dream of. Dream of which . . . Anyway! The point is, I've done it!'

And at that precise moment, his face

twitched in even more interesting ways, a little vein began to throb on his forehead, and then Lord Otherhand passed out on the floor.

Twenty minutes later, after the effective application of chocolate ice cream to the back of Valevine's neck (at Flinch's suggestion, and to Cudweed's horror) he began to stir.

One eyelid popped open, and the eye within it roamed the room, taking in the whole scene.

'Aha!' he said, and the other eye popped open. 'Yes! That's right! I'm a genius! I remember everything, except . . . Except, why do I smell of chocolate ice cream?'

He stood, gingerly at first, and then began to stroll around the Predictometer, unsure whether to play it cool and casual, or leap and dance with glee.

Suddenly he stopped.

'Whoah! Wait a minute!' he announced. 'Wait a frog-kicking moment! If it worked once, it will work again! And maybe we can be prepared for whatever weirdness this castle throws at us next. Flinch, the handle, please. Cudweed, stand well back, genius is a dangerous thing. Edgar, . . . stay where you, er, are. Right! Flinch! Hit it!'

And so once again the machine began to

spin and whirr and click and hum, and, one by one, the letters flew into place, and there we were again with another pronouncement of total wonderment.

Eek! I thought.

'Futhork!' I cried.

'Oh no!' yelled Cudweed.

'Yes!' declared Valevine, then he added, 'What? Er, what does it mean?'

But Cudweed was way ahead of him, having greater possession of the facts, and for once, I was proud of him.

'It means,' he said all in a rush, 'that we have to save Solstice! Brandish the hairy teacher is a werewolf and Solstice is trying to trap him with a leg of lamb but at this very moment she is almost certainly being eaten in large lumps and we have to try and save her or I won't have anyone to steal cookies from the kitchen for me anymore.'

'What?' roared Valevine. 'Cookies!? Werewolves?! Solstice?!'

For a moment I thought he was going to eat Cudweed himself, but somewhere deep inside that strange mind of his, the fact that his eldest offspring might be in deadly danger had got through, and his eyebrows jumped so far up his face they were lost under the mop of his hair.

'To arms!' he cried. 'To arms! Flinch! Get my elephant gun!'

'Sir, you don't have an elephant gun,' Flinch pointed out, respectfully.

'Never mind that,' he cried. 'We don't have time for excuses. Fetch my revolver!'

'But, sir, you don't have a revolver either.'

'Dammit, man! More excuses! Well, what do I have?'

Flinch thought for a moment.

'Your fishing rod?' he suggested.

'Aha! Excellent! Then bring my fishing rod. Biggest hook you can find. And a tin of worms. No! Two tins!'

And with that, we all legged it from the

lab, desperate and frantic, wondering if we could save Solstice, or whether she was already wolf food.

Seventeen
Spatchcock grows a truly impressive variety of plants and vegetables in his garden - stripy frog bushes, pendulous gnat trees, lesser-spiked barkweed. But his prize achievement every year is a pumpkin the size of a small horse.

There followed an extended period of chasing, rushing, scurrying, some flapping (that was my department), a bit more chasing, some hurrying, a touch of panicking, and after that we all ran slap bang into Valevine's back, landing in a pile of boy, butler, bird and fishing tackle on the floor of a corridor in the upper West Wing.

'Dang and drat it all!' yelled Valevine, from the bottom of the pile. 'Wait a minute!

Where are we actually going?'

Flinch picked himself out of the chaos, and helped Cudweed to get the right way up.

'Where,' Valevine repeated, 'did Solstice set her trap?'

'Well,' said Cudweed, unhooking himself. 'Right outside his room, I think.'

'Whose room?'

'The hairy werewolf's room.'

'Right then!' Off we go!'

So we set off again, storming down the corridor towards Brandish's room.

There, we saw something very uncommon indeed.

The corridor was dimly lit, just a candle in a sconce here and there. About halfway down,

floating, it seemed, in mid-air, was a leg of lamb.

'What in blue blazes . . . ?' began Valevine, and strode forwards to inspect the hanging hunk of sheep.

He reached out towards it, and at that very second, Solstice appeared from behind a curtain at the far end of the corridor.

'No! Don't touch it!' she screamed, in great panic and utmost alarm, but it was too late. Valevine had grabbed the leg of lamb.

A moment later and he had simply disappeared from view. But there was a great noise of woe and a general crashing sound, and then we all saw what had happened.

Solstice's trap had worked, it had just worked on the wrong person.

Presumably, hearing the commotion outside the door, Brandish emerged from his room.

'What's this? What's this?' he cried. 'Can't a fellow get some sleep around here?'

No one paid him any attention. We all crowded round the hole in the floor where Valevine had disappeared.

'How did you do that?' asked Cudweed, wide eyed.

Solstice was peering down into the hole

she had made.

'Father? Father, dearest? Are you dead?'

For a long moment, there was no reply, and then there came a very faint and echoing answer.

'Who turned out the lights?'

'Thank Otherhand for that!' cried Solstice, and promptly flopped down on the floor and began to cry.

'I nearly killed Father!' she sobbed.

I hopped over to her and began to peck her cheek very gently in sympathy. Cudweed and Flinch started to call down the hole, trying to make contact with Lord Otherhand, and Brandish picked his way past the pair of them and began to chastise poor Solstice.

'And just what do you think you're doing?'

he demanded.

'Ark!' I declared, pointing out that he could mind his own business.

'Well, girl?' Brandish barked. 'What do you have to say for yourself?'

Solstice stopped crying just long enough to yell at Brandish.

'It's all your fault! Because if you weren't a werewolf then you might be a nicer teacher and I wouldn't have had to get rid of you and spend the last three nights unscrewing floorboards in the corridor and how was I to know that there was a huge great drop underneath and anyway why aren't you eating us already but anyway I don't care because you're still a very nasty, horrible, unpleasant and mean old werewolf!'

Then she started crying again.

Brandish looked as though he'd been slapped with a wet octopus. He took a step back and nearly fell down the hole after all, but Flinch made a deft move and stopped him from tumbling.

'Did you say . . . werewolf?' he asked eventually.

There was a look on his face of shock and surprise, and a good deal of consternation.

Now it was Cudweed's turn. Leaving Flinch

to try and re-establish contact with Valevine, he turned on Brandish.

'Yes! You're a werewolf! Why else are you so hairy? We saw you change into a wolf! Right before our eyes!'

Brandish's mouth formed into an almost perfect circle, and his eyes opened wide. He looked more like an owl than a wolf.

'I'm no werewolf, and you are quite the most deluded pair of children I have ever met. I assure you, you are simply imagining things, and furthermore . . .'

But he was interrupted by a loud and impatient bark.

Everyone turned to see a very large and shaggy dog, the size of a Shetland pony, standing in the doorway of Brandish's room.

'Wuh!' cried Cudweed. 'Wuh-wolf!'

'Gasp!' cried Solstice.

'What's going on?' cried the voice from the hole.

Brandish's face went red, then purple, and then he turned to the dog.

'Get back in there! I thought I told you not to come out! Bad dog! Bad dog!'

'Dog?' asked Cudweed. 'Dog?'

'Mr Brandish,' said Solstice. 'Is that your dog? Your dog? Not a wolf?'

But Brandish was too busy frantically trying to get his oversized pet to obey him and go back into the room, clearly mighty embarrassed at having been caught.

Eventually he wrestled the dog back into the room, and, pointlessly pretending nothing had happened, shut the door in everyone's face.

Nasty habit, that, I thought.

'Coo,' said Cudweed, 'So let me get this straight … he's not a werewolf after all, right?'

Solstice shook her head, almost sadly, and then the disembodied voice of Lord Otherhand floated up from the gaping hole in the floorboards again.

'When,' it demanded, 'is someone going to get me out of here?!'

Eighteen

As a small boy, Valevine was quite a mischievous monkey, though you'd never guess it now. This may be because he became Lord Otherhand at a very early age, after his father was eaten by a marauding bear in the Lower Woods.

Minty stopped by the hole after an hour or so, wondering why her husband had not yet come to bed.

'Hole? Lord Otherhand? Trapped?' she said. 'I'm off to bed. Wake me if anything interesting happens.'

And away she went down the corridor in her nightie, looking very ghostly.

Solstice turned to Flinch.

'Flinch! You have to help us! How are we going to get him out of there?'

'I'm considering that, Miss Solstice,' Flinch said. 'But perhaps first a basket of provisions and some more rope would not go amiss?'

'Good idea, Best Butler!' Solstice cried, and off she went with Cudweed to fetch them.

'You go to the kitchens,' she said to Cudweed, 'and I'll get some rope. No . . . wait. Maybe I'd better go to the kitchens, and you fetch the rope. There's loads in the stables.'

And off they went, leaving Flinch and me to stare idly down into the darkness.

From time to time, Valevine would make an attempt to call up to Flinch, trying to have a brief chat, but, if there are three beings less likely to natter in the whole castle than Flinch, Valevine, and me, I should like to know who they are.

So, all in all, it was a fairly glum little scene, until I decided there was something else I could do, and, plucking up my best raven courage, I dropped down the hole to see what was what.

I think you may be aware that we ravens have pretty nifty eyesight. I can see in the dark very well, in fact, and so all I had to do was manage the particular skill of dropping vertically, controlling my descent with the odd flap of wing now and again.

The first thing I saw was that the hole underneath the floorboards was a preposterously deep one, which after a short while turned and slanted sideways for a bit, then plummeted a bit more.

I found Lord Valevine in a cramped wooden space barely big enough to contain him. He was hunched in a ball and made a little yelping noise when I dropped in to see him.

Realising he couldn't see me, not having the gift of night vision, I gave him a reassuring peck on the head.

'Rark!' I said, and he relaxed a bit.

'Oh, Edgar,' he said. 'It's you. I thought it might be a lion, or a penguin, or a goblin.'

He's a worry.

I stayed in the dark there for a bit, while Valevine found he was feeling talkative after all, and began chatting away to me. I'm afraid I fell asleep, but I do remember him talking about the castle weirdness quite a lot.

'Of course,' he said, 'there are all sorts of natural explanations for this kind of thing. Take that accident yesterday. Three kitchen maids!

Who'd have thought it? Drowned in trifle. And the business with the edible pyjama salesmen on Monday. You wouldn't think a trouser press would fall off the parapet right at that moment, would you? But I'm sure it can all be explained satisfactorily.'

He stopped for a moment, and then went on.

'But, you know, Edgar, it does rather remind me of something. Some story or other I heard when I was a boy. Ah! Young boy at large in the castle! Happy days, Edgar, happy days.'

And then I fell asleep, and I think Valevine must have too, for we spent the whole night there.

When I woke, daylight was filtering down from the corridor.

Then I noticed the end of a rope dangling into the hole, and with it, a basket containing breakfast!

I pecked Valevine, and he woke in a great flustered mess.

'Wha-whaat?' he mumbled, 'What-what? What?'

Then he saw the basket and the rope.

Ah, good, I thought. Breakfast. But what Valevine did was scramble over the basket and begin clambering up the rope in a really rather impressive manner.

I had no choice but to follow.

Halfway up, he stopped.

'Well I never!' he said loudly. Narrow as the tunnel was, I was unable to follow him, and so had to wait until he started again. I had no idea what had occurred until we both emerged gasping in the dim daylight of the morning.

There we found Cudweed, Solstice and Flinch, all fast asleep on picnic blankets, having made a loyal vigil through the night.

And now I saw the cause of Valevine's pause on his ascent from the hole.

He'd found something in that little antechamber to the hole, and it was a sort of box, a wooden cube, but broken into two pieces, which still fitted together to show how it would be when whole.

Inside the box was lined with mirrors, six of them, so that the entire interior was a set of reflections, disappearing into a black infinity.

Solstice woke first.

'Father!' she said. 'I'm so pleased you're not dead!'

'Steady girl,' warned Valevine. 'Steady.'

Cudweed woke and announced that he was hungry, and began to pick his way happily through the basket, which Valevine had pulled up after him.

'Gasp!' said Solstice next. 'What's that?'

'Useless box I found in the hole,' Valevine said. 'Though still, it does remind me of something . . .'

But his thoughts were interrupted by the

appearance of Minty drifting along to see how things were going.

'Ah, husband,' she said. 'You're not dead. I'm so pleased. Now, will someone please explain what is going on here? Hmm? I'm waiting . . .'

Well, that someone was Solstice, who launched into a long and rather confused account of the situation, involving sheep's legs, werewolves, hairy teachers, rope, trapdoors, a deep hatred of geography homework, and hidden dogs.

At the end of all this, which Minty had taken on board without so much as raising a single eyebrow, not one, she merely had one question.

'Did you say that Mr Brandish is secretly keeping a large and hairy hound in his room?'

Solstice nodded.

'Right!' declared Minty, suddenly managing to look rather terrifying in her nightgown. 'You know the policy on pets in this castle! I will not have stowaway canines in the castle. We have been deceived!'

She began to knock fiercely on Brandish's door.

'Mr Brandish! Mr Brandish! Open this door immediately if you please! I am going to have to ask you to leave the castle. Immediately!

Mr Brandish, will you open this door?'

And with that, Solstice and Cudweed turned to each other and whooped for joy.

The whooping was too much for Valevine, and Flinch, who shuffled off back to the lab, Lord Otherhand muttering something about firewood as he went.

'Yay!' cried Solstice. 'We did it, after all!'

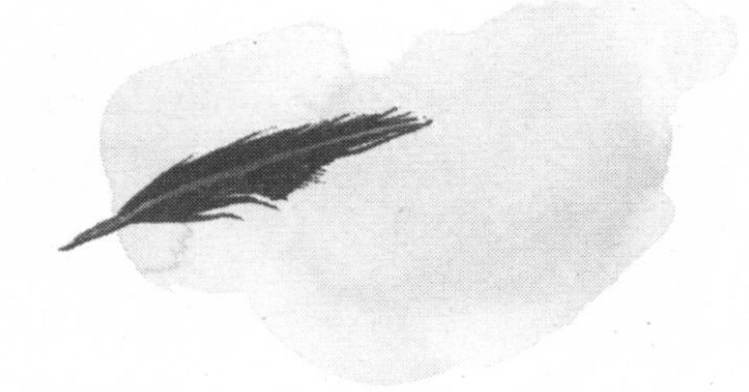

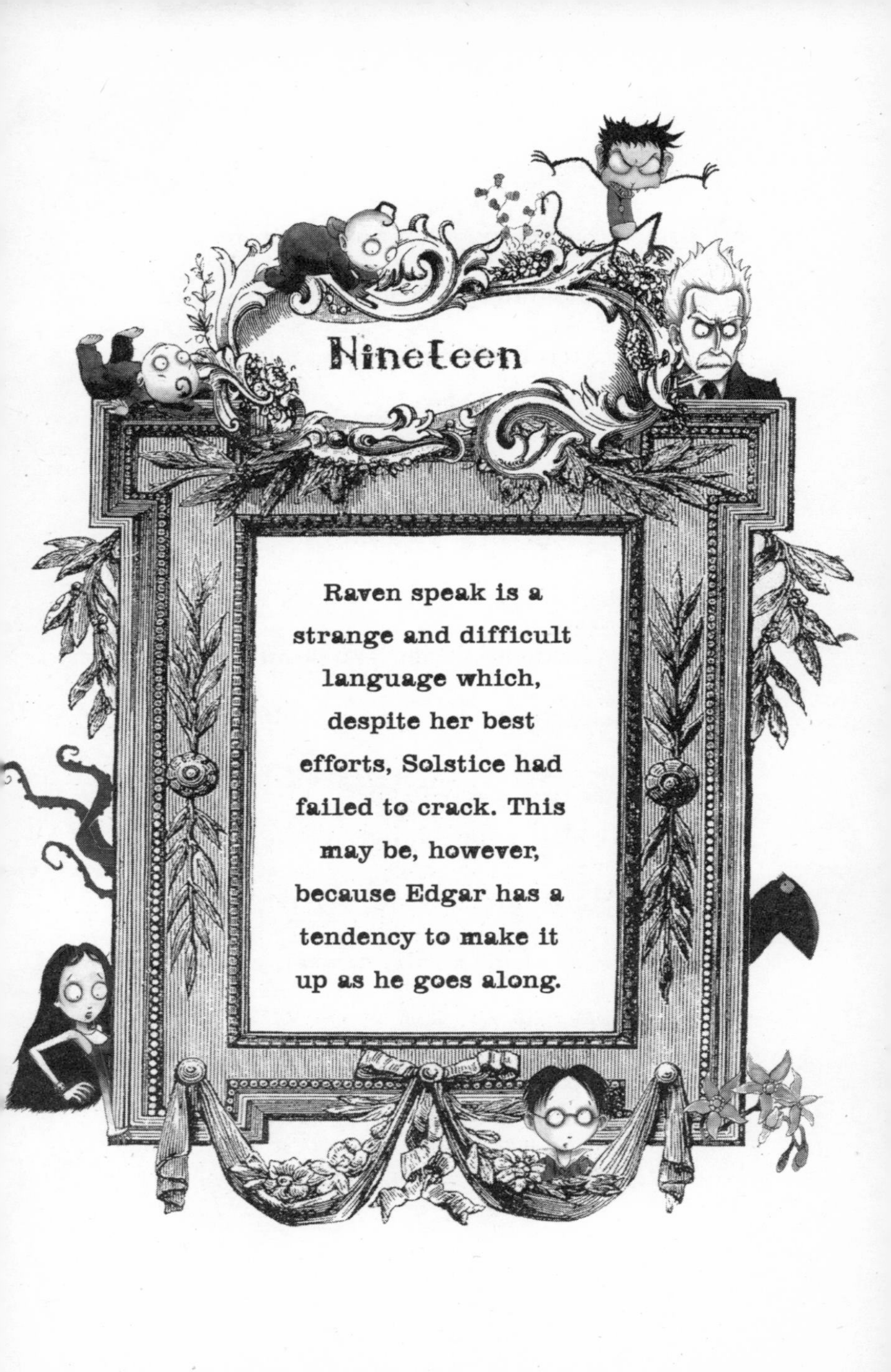

Nineteen

Raven speak is a strange and difficult language which, despite her best efforts, Solstice had failed to crack. This may be, however, because Edgar has a tendency to make it up as he goes along.

Minty gave Mr Brandish till lunchtime to pack his things and go. It all made sense now, the big crate he'd arrived with, full not of clothes or text books, but a very large Norwegian Elkhound. Sheepishly, Mr Brandish explained his predicament.

'It's . . . my wife, you see,' he said. 'She wouldn't put up with Felicity any more.'

Felicity, I realised, was the dog's name.

'She got very angry . . . you don't know what she's like . . .' he said, trembling like a cold pigeon. 'She told me Felicity had to go. It's either her, or me, she said! So off we went, and I've been on the go ever since.'

He told a tale of a life on the road, and everywhere he went it was always the same, Felicity would get him into trouble, and so he'd decided to try and keep her a secret when he came for the job at Castle Otherhand.

So one half of the crisis at Castle Otherhand was sorted, but there was still the matter of the freakishly dangerous outbreaks of ill luck that were occurring on an ever more frequent basis.

And yet, even this oh-so-imponderable issue was soon to be solved, and, ahem, I may say, somewhat immodestly, that your old friend Edgar had no small part to play in the solution.

It went like this.

There was an almighty yell from the topmost balcony of the Small Hall.

'View-hallooo!' came the call, so far away and distant as to be almost indistinct, but nevertheless,

I knew it to be the call of Lord Otherhand.

'Look out there! Below! Look out below!'

Now he went on in this way for a good five minutes, until half the castle was gathered on the ground floor of the Small Hall.

'Look out, I say! Look out! Clear the area, clear the area!'

Finally someone decided to call back up to Valevine.

It was Minty having come to see what all the fuss was about.

'We are clear! What on earth is going on?'

'Look out! Look out below.'

'Oh, for the sake of . . .' sighed Minty, but then, the mystery was over.

Craning our necks up to the gallery way

above our heads, we saw the sight of a piano gradually being winched out into the space above the Small Hall. Or at least, it looked like a piano at first, but then we realised that it was in fact, the ex-piano, the Predictometer.

'Wait! Father!' cried Solstice from below, 'What are you doing? It works. It actually works! Why do you want to destroy it? It works!'

Valevine answered from above, though he did not stop winching.

'It does not work, oh daughter of mine. It appeared to have worked, but do I need to tell you, of all people, that you were not eaten by the teacher, hairy or otherwise? And thus we can deduce that the whole thing has been a monumental waste of time.'

'At last,' muttered Minty, 'he's seen sense.'

'But maybe it just needs a bit more fixing,' Cudweed said. 'Maybe it's nearly right. You were nearly eaten by a werewolf, weren't you? Sort of,' he added, turning to Solstice.

But it was not to be, for at that moment, with another monumental cry of 'Look out there!' the piano-Predictometer began its graceful descent to the floor below.

I flew shrieking into the air, as the thing, oddly quietly, fell almost the entire height of the castle, and landed with the greatest possible noise and mess on the Small Hall floor.

It disintegrated almost entirely. I say almost, because, as Valevine and Flinch hurried downstairs like eager schoolboys, desperate to see the extent of the damage, we all saw that there was one part of the machine still intact, namely, the display.

And upon it was written these words:

Stupid Lord remembers Otherhand Luck Diamond.

'What . . .' pondered Solstice slowly, 'what do you suppose that means?'

There was an embarrassed shuffling behind us, and a small cough, and we turned to see Lord Valevine looking bemused.

'Well, I, er . . .' he muttered, 'that is, I seem to find it all making some kind of sense now. Heh. And I find myself somewhat, er, remiss. Yes, it all makes sense. The diamond thing. The mirrored box. The oddness and weirdness. Oh dear,' he said. 'I think I owe you all an explanation.'

Twenty

Castle Otherhand is an old mysterious place, and so big that there are many rooms that have simply been forgotten about. One such is the Round Room, a perfectly spherical room created by Mad Monty, the fourth Lord Otherhand.

It was an unlikely tale, at best.

In fact, it was the most unlikely story we had ever heard, and yet that was precisely the point.

Now at last, Valevine had remembered the legend of the Luck of Otherhand. Part of the fabulous and somewhat mythical treasure supposed to be hidden somewhere around the castle, the Luck of Otherhand was a single solitaire diamond the size of a good raven's head at least, but which, despite its obvious and enormous value, was cursed.

'Yes,' explained Valevine. 'It was said that the Luck of Otherhand was cursed with the power to cause extraordinarily unlikely things to happen all around it. All the time it was in the castle, general and frequently dangerously odd things would happen. The family, figuring this out, decided it had to be got rid of. But the trouble is that according to the legend, the Luck could not just be given or thrown away, or its power would remain, good and bad. Mostly bad.

'So finally, according to the legend, I mean, if you think it's true, some Lord Otherhand or other made a mirrored box, and hid the diamond inside. Somehow the mirrors kept the Luck inside, and stopped the weirdness. And then they hid it somewhere in the castle.

'And so,' finished Valevine, looking more sheepish than ever, 'we must conclude that the diamond, having clearly been set free from the box made to trap it, is wreaking its havoc once more.'

And if Valevine was sheepish, I said nothing, for I was feeling even more sheepish myself. For I too knew the legend of the Luck of Otherhand, and if I didn't look totally guilty myself for not thinking of it first, it was because you can't see a raven blush. It's to do with feathers, you see.

'But,' said Solstice, 'that is all so very unlikely! The whole thing. Right from the start, right up to you finding the broken box.'

Valevine nodded, and a wicked grin began to seep back into his face.

'Yes, my girl, but that is exactly what the diamond does. It causes the weirdest of weird things to happen. There is no escape from its logic. But as to why it's all happening again now, heaven only knows!'

'Ah!' cried Solstice. 'I have it! Yes, I have it. The earthquake! It all began with the earthquake.'

'That's it!' cried Valevine. 'The earthquake must have dislodged the box, placed in that secret passage that you uncovered. With the box broken, the Luck could wreak its unholy power once more!'

'But where is it now?' asked Solstice. 'It wasn't in the hole, was it?'

'Indeed, not,' said Valevine. 'But I'll tell you this, wherever there is the greatest concentration of strange and utterly unlikely things happening, then that's where we'll find the diamond.'

'Well,' said a small voice, and everyone turned to look at Cudweed, whose small voice it was. 'That's easy. It's my monkey.'

Twenty-one

When Edgar was a young raven, he regularly flew a hundred miles a day without even thinking about it. Now he thinks twice about whether it's actually worth getting up in the morning. It often isn't.

Futhork

The chubby boy was right. It all made sense now. The day of the earthquake, Fellah running away over the rooftops, disappearing into the castle, he must have found the diamond and returned with it clutched in one hand, looking as if he was limping, back to some hidden lair in the castle. And I say that he found the diamond, but maybe, oh brain-bending thought, maybe it was the diamond that found him . . .

Whatever the answer to such questions, we all immediately agreed that Cudweed was right.

And so began an infamous episode in Otherhand history, namely, the Great Monkey Hunt of Castle Otherhand.

The entire castle was involved. Everyone,

from the lowliest bootboy to Lord Otherhand himself, and the only person who did not take an active part in the hunt was Grandma Slivinkov, who was too frail to do much hunting. She did, however, seem to catch the general mood of excitement, and kept asking people if we were going to eat the monkey once we'd caught it, much to Cudweed's dismay. And my pleasure.

The Monkey Hunt caused such an uproar and commotion in the Castle as has not been seen since the last time that something vaguely dangerous happened, but I have to confess, that it was Solstice who put her finger on the problem, when she said,

'Do you know, I bet Edgar can find Fellah, without even trying. He must have the best sense of smell of any of us!'

And she was right, and the only reason I hadn't volunteered myself was that I do not like sniffing monkeys, as a rule. But the times called for desperate measures, and so, while everyone else fruitlessly ran from the top of the castle to the bottom, and back again, Solstice told Cudweed to fetch something of Fellah's, and he came back with the monkey's blanket.

Now, I don't know if you can imagine smelling a monkey's blanket,

but let me assure you, to a bird such as me with a deadly keen sense of smell, it was rather like inhaling a dungheap.

'Have you got it?' Solstice urged. 'Yes? Do you need another sniff?'

'Futhork!' I squawked. No I did not. And to prove it, I set off at a frantic pace through the castle, if only to get some wind whistling through the old beak and clear out that infernal stink.

Solstice, Cudweed, and then one by one, everyone else, set off after me, as I wound my way this way and that through the castle, and do you know, I found that monkey in fifteen minutes.

A little slow, maybe, but I'm not as young as I used to be.

The monkey was cowering in an attic,

surrounded on all
sides by evidence
of the weirdness.
He was
once again
imaginatively
dressed, this
time as a little
green gnome,
complete with
pointy hat and
boots. Around
him, a family
of mice were
performing as if
they were born

to the circus, making a little pyramid of mouseness on the floor in front of him.

Fellah again looked faintly bewildered by everything, not least the sudden arrival in his seceret hideout of almost everyone in the place. Clutched in one paw, glinting and gleaming, was the largest, sparkliest and most valuable diamond

ever to be seen, and at that moment, about twenty-three pairs of hands all dived for the monkey at once, sending mice squeaking away in terror, even though their show was only halfway through.

Valevine called a castle meeting, in the Small Hall.

'Well, then,' he said, tossing the diamond from hand to hand as though it was a grenade. 'Any ideas what we do with this? Anyone?'

'Keep it!' said Cudweed. 'It's got to be worth a fortune.'

'It would rather solve our money worries, dear,' whispered Minty to her husband, so the serving staff wouldn't hear.

'Keep us in kitchen maids for quite a while, eh?' agreed Valevine. 'Maybe even pay for some repairs on the old place, what? But no! It cannot be! Do you want to live with this level of chaos all the time? And the random and spectacularly unlikely deaths? I think not.'

Minty sighed, nodding.

'Then the only answer is to give it away,' said Solstice. 'Or throw it in the lake!'

'Back to school for you, my girl!' chided Valevine. 'Do you not remember the part of the legend which says that it may neither be given away or otherwise disposed of, or the Luck would stay?'

As if on cue, at the mention of school, Brandish appeared in the Hall, his large and now very un-secret dog behind him, a small travelling bag under one arm.

'No,' Valevine continued. 'There are only two options. Either we repair the box and hide the thing once more. Or we find someone to willingly buy it from us. The legend says nothing about that.'

'Hmm,' said Minty. 'I like the second option better. I'd never feel safe knowing it was lurking in the building, ready to strike again. And at least we could make some money . . . but who on earth is going to buy that thing from us?'

And then came the very final, but by now highly commonplace, un-commonplace thing. There was a bash on the door, and Flinch opening it was fairly

knocked aside by the entrance of a very large, that is to say fat, and tall, lady.

She had a look on her face like thunder and when she saw Brandish putting his coat on, she went ballistic. Absolutely mental.

'Melvin!' she shrieked, barging her way into the Small Hall without a by your leave. 'Melvin Brandish! How dare you just run off with that mutt and leave me high and dry?'

'Hello, dear,' sighed Brandish, suddenly very meek indeed. 'Everyone, please meet my wife . . .'

'Don't you "everyone" me,' declared Mrs B. 'You get your coat on and get out of this place at once, do you hear? I won't have it, I simply won't . . .'

And with that she suddenly broke off, and stared hard at Valevine. Or to be more precise, she stared hard at the Luck, which he was still tossing about like a tennis ball.

'What . . . ?' she said. 'What on earth? What on earth is that?'

'What is this?' enquired Valevine. 'This is the famous Luck of Otherhand. The most fabulous diamond known to man or raven. Why do you ask?'

'Because I simply must have it,' Mrs B announced, starting to scare everyone slightly.

'Mrs Brandish collects rare diamonds,' her husband explained weakly to no one in particular. 'It gets quite . . . expensive.'

'Is that so?' asked Valevine, slyly. 'Is that, how shall I put it, so?'

But Mrs B was by now hypnotised by the sight of the Luck.

'Melvin,' she yelled. 'Get your cheque book out!'

So it was that the most ridiculously improbable sequence of events that had ever occurred was put to an end to by one more impossibly impossible chance event: the arrival of a collector of rare gemstones at just the right moment.

As the door swung shut behind Mr and Mrs B, and Felicity, and they made their argumentative way off down the driveway, Valevine chuckled to himself, folding a rather sizeable cheque into four and placing it in his top pocket.

Solstice, Cudweed and I made our way up to the High Terrace, eager to see that the Brandish clan were well and truly leaving the premises.

'I don't get it,' said Cudweed. 'None of that makes any sense. At all.'

'No,' agreed Solstice, 'but I think that's the point.'

'Oh,' said Cudweed. 'I see.'

He clearly didn't.

But it didn't matter.

'**Ark!**' I said.

'What's that, Edgar?' Solstice asked, but then she saw for herself.

Because just as Mr and Mrs Brandish made their way under the last gateway, and back on the main road to the big wide world, a very large and very dangerous portacabin fell out of the sky and squashed them flat, leaving a bemused but quite happy Felicity to scamper off into the woods,

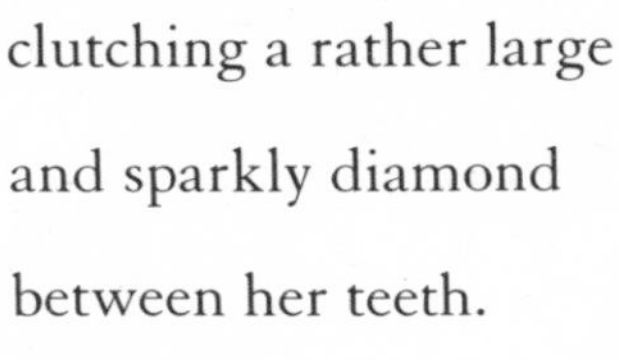

clutching a rather large and sparkly diamond between her teeth.

'Gasp,' said Solstice.

'Coo,' said Cudweed. 'What are the chances of that happening?'

'Oh, for goodness' sake, Cudweed,' moaned Solstice. 'Don't start that again!'

And I could only agree.

'**Arrrrk!**'

Postscript

It should be noted that although Valevine was pleased with the size of the cheque he brandished from Mr Brandish, his pleasure was short-lived, for the cheque bounced when he tried to cash it in at the bank.

There then ensued a long and unsuccessful search for the Luck, that fabulously valuable, yet ill-starred, gem. Nevertheless, we were comforted by the thought that the vast bulk of the missing hoard of Otherhand treasure still remained somewhere in the castle. Unfound, for now.

Fellah was not so lucky, for having scampered round the remains of the portacabin for twenty minutes, he was caught by Cudweed, who promptly took him off for a bath, remarking once again, that nobody likes a sticky monkey.

Edgar spreads his wings in . . .

Flood and Fang

Ghosts and Gadgets

. . . he ruffles his feathers in . . .

Lunatics and Luck

. . . reveals more Otherhand family secrets in . . .

Vampires and Volts coming in time for Halloween 2010

Magic and Mayhem in March 2011

and swoops in for more feathery antics in . . .

Diamonds and Doom coming in October 2011

Is my beak wonky? Am I going grey? At the very least I suspect I may have fleas again.

But no matter, I, Edgar, Guardian of the Castle, long-standing protector of the endlessly stupid Otherhand family, and fine example of ravens everywhere, am proud to present this most wonderful piece of modern technology. Not another useless invention from his Lordship, I hear you ask? No, this actually works.

To find out more about The Raven Mysteries books, read my blog, explore the Castle, meet the family, search for the lost treasure of Otherhand, and much more, visit . . .

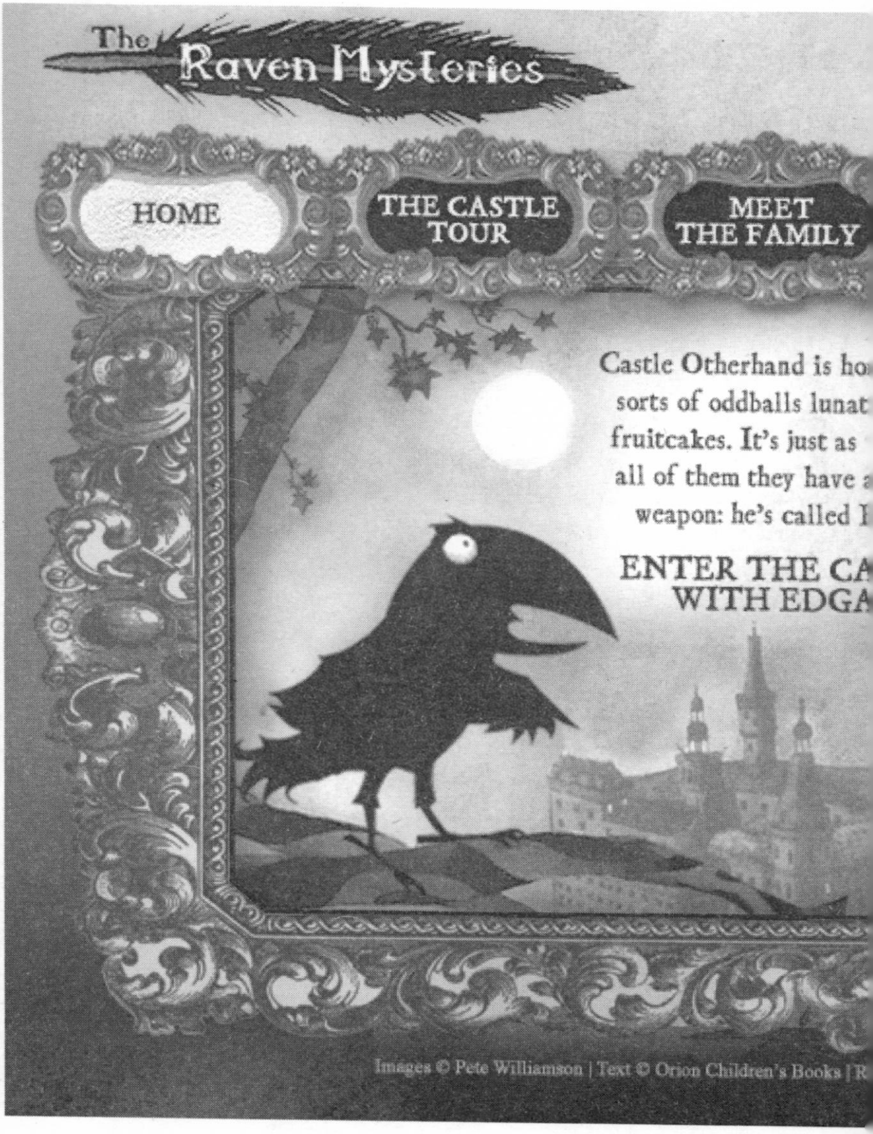
The Raven Mysteries
HOME
THE CASTLE TOUR
MEET THE FAMILY
Castle Otherhand is
sorts of oddballs
fruitcakes. It's just as
all of them they have
weapon: he's called
ENTER THE
WITH
Images © Pete Williamson | Text © Orion Children's Books |

oth Froth Members
Entry Gate:

EMAIL

LOG-IN

THE BOOKS

GOTH-FROTH

EVENTS

SOLSTICE'S BEAUTY REGIME

How to look gothicly gorgeous

CLICK HERE

LATEST BOOK

'FLOOD AND FANG'

FIND OUT MORE»

COMING SOON!

FELLAH VS EDGAR

Much pecking and pulling of feathers

PLAY NOW

orybook text © Marcus Sedgewick | Sitemap | Accessibility

The Raven Mysteries

HOME

THE CASTLE TOUR

MEET THE FAMILY

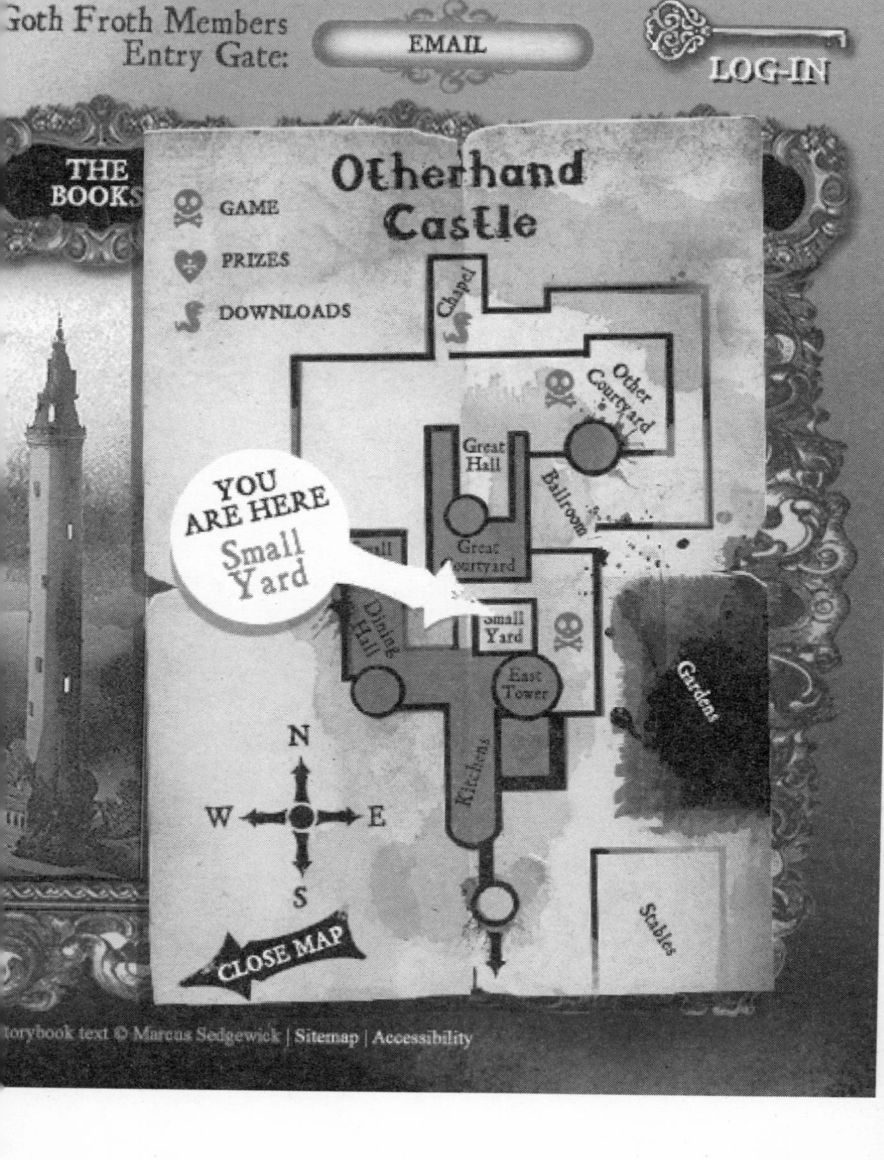

Goth Froth Members Entry Gate:
EMAIL
LOG-IN
THE BOOKS
Otherhand Castle
GAME
PRIZES
DOWNLOADS
Chapel
Other Courtyard
Great Hall
Ballroom
YOU ARE HERE
Small Yard
Great Courtyard
Dining Hall
Small Yard
East Tower
Gardens
Kitchens
N
W
E
S
Stables
CLOSE MAP
torybook text © Marcus Sedgewick | Sitemap | Accessibility